She woke to the weight of a male leg thrown over her

Phoebe's eyes flew open. Her. Ryan. Entwined. They'd started out on opposite sides of the bed last night. But this morning they'd definitely found themselves in the middle.

The sensible thing would be to extricate herself immediately. And she would—in just a minute. What harm could possibly come from a few minutes of sensual indulgence?

She closed her eyes and absorbed the feel of him. The muscular length of his legs tangled with hers. The tease of his springy chest hair against her bared breast. The ripple of his belly beneath her hand. The hard ridge of his erection pressed against her thigh...

She knew he wanted her as desperately as she wanted him. She'd seen it in the heat in his eyes, heard the hoarse want in his voice.

Languid, liquid desire flowed through her, filled her. Nestled in his arms, Phoebe realized she'd never truly known desire before. What she'd thought was desire had been merely sexual arousal.

Ryan was her desire.

Too bad he was also

Dear Reader,

What do you do when you and your best friend—your
male best friend—find yourselves dumped by your
dates at a couples-only resort on a tropical island? If
you're supercompetitive Phoebe Matthews, you save
face by pretending to be madly in lust with your best
friend, sexy Ryan Palmer. It shouldn't be a big deal for
these best friends to share a room and pretend they're
wildly attracted to each other. But…throw in a little
island magic and a potent sexual attraction that's been
brewing for years and things get hot, hot, hot!

Can laid-back Ryan, who changes girlfriends as
frequently as some men change ESPN channels,
and Phoebe, who has an excessive need for stability,
indulge in a sex, sun and sand fling and still salvage
a friendship that means everything to both of them?

I loved writing about Ryan and Phoebe—two people
who head to a tropical isle looking for love and
discover it's been right in front of them all along.
I hope you enjoy their *Barely Decent* escapades
in Jamaica. I'd love to hear from you if you do.
Unfortunately, you won't find me in the Islands. But
you can write to me at P.O. Box 801068, Acworth, GA
30101.

Enjoy the heat,

Jennifer LaBrecque

Books by Jennifer LaBrecque

HARLEQUIN TEMPTATION
886—BARELY MISTAKEN

HARLEQUIN DUETS
28—ANDREW IN EXCESS
52—KIDS + COPS = CHAOS
64—JINGLE BELL BRIDE?

Barely Decent
Jennifer LaBrecque

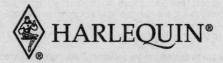

HARLEQUIN®

TORONTO • NEW YORK • LONDON
AMSTERDAM • PARIS • SYDNEY • HAMBURG
STOCKHOLM • ATHENS • TOKYO • MILAN • MADRID
PRAGUE • WARSAW • BUDAPEST • AUCKLAND

In memory of Carol Mann Arnold, who loved Howard,
her family, Hannah Banana, pinochle, golf,
hickory taters, pink dogwoods and life.
You taught me to believe in angels.

ISBN 0-373-69104-1

BARELY DECENT

Copyright © 2002 by Jennifer LaBrecque.

Visit us at www.eHarlequin.com

Printed in U.S.A.

_____Prologue_____

"I DON'T CARE if he _did_ ask you to the prom, he's just trying to get in your pants. Bobby's a player." Ryan Palmer stood in front of his best friend, Phoebe Matthews, his arms crossed over his chest, his chin jutting at a stubborn angle, a classic case of the pot calling the kettle black. Except it had never occurred to Ryan to try to get into her pants, and Bobby wasn't a player—just a quiet guy who'd developed a crush on her.

"According to you, they're all players or dweebs or punks or something. Anyway, he invited me to the prom, not a hotel room." Heat crept up Phoebe's face as she toed the swing into motion, forcing Ryan to step back or suffer a whacked shin. She felt like whacking him upside the head. "For crying out loud, Ryan, all he did was kiss me and ask me out."

She was probably the only eighteen-year-old girl in their entire school—possibly the entire planet—who'd never been kissed until today. Mainly, she figured, because outspoken, tall, flat-chested brainiacs didn't exactly have boys lining up to kiss them. But also, because Ryan had taken on the misguided, self-appointed position of watchdog over her virtue. And because her best friend, Ryan, was the chief eighteen-year-old boy *doing* the kissing. And best friends didn't kiss. Did they?

So Phoebe had come up with a plan, and when Bobby Richmond had whipped out his ChapStick, primed his lips and laid one on her, she'd been ready. Kissing Bobby had been a little waxy—actually a lot waxy—but okay, until thoughts of Ryan had popped in her head and she'd wondered if kissing Ryan would be more than okay.

Phoebe studied Ryan from where she sat on the swing. Average build. Stocky. Sandy blond hair. Jade green eyes. Ryan wasn't the best-looking boy in school or the smartest or the most athletic, but he possessed something far more potent. Aunt Caroline called it charm and charisma. Whatever "it" was, he had it. Girls had been dropping at his feet since elementary school.

"I'll have a little talk with Bobby Richmond."

"Do it and die." Phoebe swung a little harder. "Don't get all bent out of shape about a kiss. A kiss is nothing when you consider there are girls in school having babies."

"Phoebes—"

A little shock was good for him now and then. "I don't want to have a baby, you nut. But a kiss and a date to my senior prom don't seem like too much to ask. Thanks to my flat chest and your 'talks' with every guy who even looked my way, I'm blooming plenty late without any additional help from you."

She handed him the perfect opportunity to pull out

that charm he plied all the other girls with—curvy, busty, petite, cute girls—and insist that her flat chest and gangly legs weren't important. She awaited his response, her heart pounding far harder than when Bobby had laid his ChapStick-coated lips on hers.

"But, Phoebes, you don't know guys the way I know guys." Ryan shoved his hands in his blue jean pockets and looked everywhere except the vicinity of her chest. Had the subject of her nonexistent chest embarrassed him, the King of the Casanovas? Was that what had brought on this awkward tension between them?

She looked past him to the azaleas blooming outside the screened porch, embarrassment radiating through her. Toulouse, one of Aunt Caroline's numerous adopted stray cats, sunned himself by the porch steps.

Slightly bruised, her heart slowed to its normal rate. So much for the silly notion Ryan might see her as more than a friend. She was just feeling uncertain with all the changes looming around the corner. High school graduation. College in the fall. Would she and Ryan remain close? Or would he meet some girl at college and no longer need her friendship?

"Sure I know guys. You're a guy. I've got the inside scoop on that dark hole known as the male mind. That's why I had to come up with a plan."

Ryan groaned and ran his hand through his cropped hair. "Not another one of your plans?"

So, once in a blue moon her plans went slightly awry, like that fourth grade science experiment. Ryan needed to get over that. His hair had only been pink for a day or two.

"Plans make perfect sense." Plans were important. Phoebe had already planned the next ten years while Ryan was still trying to decide on a college major.

"You've got to learn to go with the flow, Phoebes."

"If you make a plan, you should stick with it." She glared at him, daring him to disagree.

The front door opened. Aunt Caroline stepped onto the porch, the two calico cats, Lilly and Millie, trailing behind. "Sugar, I'm running up to the store. I want to make that chocolate torte you like so much for your graduation party and we need cat food. Uncle Frank's in his studio. He's having a hard time with this piece of stone, so you might want to steer clear."

In the twelve years Phoebe had lived with them, she'd learned not to disturb her uncle when he was sculpting in his studio. Give Uncle Frank—a nice, reasonable man—a chisel and a stone slab, and he morphed into Mr. Hyde.

Lilly twined between Ryan's legs. Millie found Phoebe's lap and kneaded before finally curling into place.

Aunt Caroline blew across the porch and out the screen door, letting it slam behind her. "Do you need anything? Ryan, are you staying for dinner?"

"I don't need anything." Phoebe absently scratched behind Millie's ears. She double-checked the driveway two houses down. "Your dad's not home." Ryan didn't bother to look.

"Sure, I'll stay for dinner." Ryan seldom turned down an invitation. Mostly because he never knew whether his father and his father's latest girlfriend would be around. But Phoebe knew he joined them more for the company than the food.

Caroline paused on the last stone step, looking at Phoebe. "Lynette called this afternoon." Phoebe's stomach lurched, as it always did when anyone mentioned her mother's name. "She and Vance can't make your graduation, after all." Caroline's voice carried, soft and apologetic, in the spring afternoon, the same as every time she broke the news that once again Phoebe's parents would be no-shows.

Twelve years ago, Phoebe and her parents had driven to Nashville from Florida, where they lived from town to town. Lynette and Vance had dropped their daughter off for a "visit" with her aunt Caroline and uncle Frank. Phoebe hadn't seen them since. They'd never came back. Phoebe lost count of the number of times they had promised to come and never showed up.

Relief warred with anger. Relief that she wouldn't have to see them. Anger, once again, that they had passed her on like a useless piece of furniture. She kept her expression neutral and her voice steady. "I didn't really expect them. But thanks for letting me know."

Aunt Caroline paused and then jammed her sunglasses on over angry, sympathetic eyes. "I won't be gone long." She hadn't walked out the door without uttering that reassurance since the day she'd given up her job as a flight attendant after six-year-old Phoebe had freaked out over her two-day absence.

Desperately trying to swallow the lump lodged in her throat, Phoebe watched her aunt climb into her car. Dammit, she'd thought that since she was valedictorian, just this once her parents might... Couldn't they ever follow through on anything? "It's important to make plans and stick with them."

Ryan dropped beside her, setting the swing in motion again. He pulled her close, his hand smoothing her hair in a familiar gesture of comfort. The same way he'd comforted her twelve years ago when he'd found her crying in the woods behind his house, when she'd finally figured out her parents weren't coming back for her. The same way she'd comforted him when he'd told her his mother drank herself to death months before. "They're idiots, Phoebe."

She looked at him. Her tears, held at bay, blurred his features. She recognized the pain rippling through him. Every time her parents let her down, Ryan lost his mother all over again. She repeated the comfort they'd offered each other throughout childhood. "We can't choose our parents, but we can choose our friends. And I choose you."

She settled her head against his shoulder and squelched the shiver of girlish longing that chased down her spine at the contact. Boyfriends came and went, but friends were forever.

1

Twelve years later

"So, WHAT do you think?" Phoebe pushed the glossy, trifold brochure across the pub-style tabletop. She already knew what Ryan would think of the photos promising white sugar beaches, clear blue water, more aqua sports than she could count and sizzling tropical nights.

Ryan pointedly glanced out the restaurant window at the slushy sidewalks and heavy gray skies.

"The temperature in Nashville's barely going to crawl above freezing for the rest of this week." A slow grin revealed the dimple that had broken hearts since grade school. "Sun, sand and sex. What's not to like?" He flicked the brochure with his finger, "What's the occasion?"

"It's a celebration of sorts." She paused, smoothing her hand over her red suit jacket. "You are looking at the new marketing director for Capshaw and Griffen. It comes with a window office and a nice fat salary increase."

"Hot damn, Phoebes. That's great. You got it." He high-fived her across the table. Genuine happiness crinkled the corners of his eyes and pulled his dimples into full play.

Even after all these years as friends, her heart pounded a little harder when he smiled that way. "I couldn't wait to tell you." She'd forced herself not to call him on her cell phone, wanting to share the good news in person.

"You deserve it. You've worked your butt off for eight years and you're brilliant. They're damn lucky to have you. How'd Charlie take it?"

Poor Ryan. How many weekly lunches had he suffered through her trials and tribulations with her nemesis, Charlie Langley? About the same number she'd suffered through his change of girlfriends.

"Charlie didn't take it well." Phoebe nibbled at the end of her bread stick. "He and Skip Griffen were Lambda Chi brothers. He pretty much considered the promotion his for the asking. He resigned this morning when they made the announcement. Good riddance, if you ask me."

"Damn straight. He made your life hell for the last couple of years. I'd like to have met him in a dark alley more than once," Ryan grumbled, always ready to champion her.

"Nah. It was much sweeter this way. He should've never underestimated a woman with a plan." She forked her olives onto her bread plate and slid it across the table to him.

"A plan and a competitive streak a mile wide make

for an overachiever. Let me guess, you're the youngest marketing director in the history of the company."

She couldn't suppress a grin. "By two years. And you're one to talk about overachievers, Mr. Top Salesman in the southeast for Rooker Sports Equipment."

Ryan devoured the olives, taking her comeback in stride. He knew his accomplishments meant as much to her as her own. "This fat salary increase…how fat?"

"Do I make more money than you? Is that the question?" She shook her head, teasing. "I'll never tell."

"You know I could catch you with your shoes off and tickle it out of you."

"You'd be a dead man. Let's just say I'm catching up to you fast. So, do you and a date want to come to Jamaica with me and Elliott?" She lined up the proper balance of lettuce, tomato and feta on the tines of her fork. "Come on. It'll be so much more fun if you're there. By the way, who *is* the girlfriend de jour?"

"Her name's Kiki. And she's a very nice girl."

"Uh-huh. They all are." And they were. Even after he moved on to the next one, they remained friendly. One big happy harem. It never ceased to amaze and annoy her. "You change girlfriends the way some men change ESPN channels."

Ryan quirked one sandy eyebrow, devilment lighting his pale green eyes. "There's lots of good sports, Phoebes. You stay on one channel too long and you miss something on another one."

That was no way to approach a relationship. Phoebe shook her head. She worried about Ryan and his steady stream of vacuous relationships. "What do you talk about with these nice, but let's face it, not very bright women you tend to favor?"

"Are you saying a smart woman wouldn't want to date me?"

A sexy, captivating man with the attention span of a gnat? He made a wonderful friend—considerate, caring, dependable, fun—but she'd watched him over the years, and he didn't extend the same effort as a boyfriend.

"Absolutely. No woman in her right mind would go out with a man who changes channels as often as you do."

Ryan's smile qualified as wicked. "Maybe I've got a really impressive channel changer."

A purely feminine response shivered down her spine at his sexy suggestion, setting off a clamor of warning bells in her head. No way she'd ever tell him she'd wondered about his channel changer on the odd occasion, late at night, in the privacy of her bedroom. Channel changers, impressive or not, didn't belong in a friendship. "Don't go there. And don't try to switch the subject." Phoebe stabbed her fork in his direction. "What *do* you talk about?"

Actually, she was terribly curious. What allure did these women have other than the obvious physical appeal? Sex only carried a relationship so far.

Ryan shrugged. "Stuff. I'm not looking for deep conversation from a girlfriend—"

"Good. You'd be out of luck." Well, that sounded nice and bitchy. Even if it was true.

"If I want to discuss world peace, I've got you."

Sometimes they talked for hours on end about everything and nothing. And sometimes they spent hours together with only comfortable silence between them.

"I've been thinking about it. I've decided you're emotionally retarded, and I think I'm an enabler." She was only half teasing. Was their friendship part of the reason he drifted in and out of relationships? If she were a male friend instead of a female one, would he look for a deeper relationship with some of the women he merely skimmed the surface with? It was a painful thought.

"I'm a guy. I'm supposed to be emotionally retarded."

She hated it when he refused to take her seriously. "You do a good job of it. Go ahead and laugh. One day someone's going to break your heart. Big time."

"Nah. It'll never happen."

"How can you be so sure?"

"You change the channel before you get that interested in the outcome of the game." Ryan sliced off a neat quarter of his stromboli and shifted it to an empty salad plate, stringing melted cheese along the way. "Anyway, in the unlikely event that transpires, I've always got you to pick up the pieces, Ms. Enabler."

Just as she'd always been able to count on him. Phoebe brushed aside the niggling thought that a part of her liked the fact that he never had a serious relationship with another woman.

He shoved the plate across the table. It dinged against her water glass. "You sure Kiki and I won't cramp Geek Boy's style if we tag along to this couples-only resort?"

Her mouth watered as steam rose from the cheese-and spinach-filled dough. She preferred the stromboli, but the salad made her feel better about her waistline management. So each week she ordered what she needed, and Ryan parceled out a portion of what she really wanted.

"I'm sure *Elliott* won't mind when I mention it." And it would be so much more fun with Ryan along. And Kiki.

"He doesn't even know yet, does he?" Ryan laughed and shook his head. "You're something else. You'll just set everything up and then give him the dates he's supposed to show up?"

"Something like that." Ryan often razzed her about her take-charge personality. "He's close to tenure now and very busy."

"Do the two of you ever discuss anything *other* than world peace?" Ryan turned the tables on her.

An associate professor of Greek and Roman literature at Vanderbilt University, Elliott took himself very seriously.

"Occasionally." Actually, Elliott was so reflective, a touch of frivolity would be nice. "We both need a break." She hoped the break jump-started their stagnant relationship. He was sweating his upcoming review, and she'd been working her buns off to land this promotion. A little R and R should do them both a world of good.

Naomi, their regular waitress, stopped by. "The stromboli okay?" Ryan gave her a thumbs up. "Good. You two splitting a baklava today?"

Beach? Bathing suit? Baklava? "No."

"Yes. One baklava. Two forks," Ryan countermanded. Naomi grinned as she walked away.

Ryan affected women that way. Young. Old. It didn't matter. He charmed them all. She thanked the powers that be—and not for the first time—that she fell under the best friend immunity umbrella.

"One bite." She'd allow herself a taste of the honey-and walnut-filled pastry. "Stop me at one bite." Phoebe eased back on the wooden seat, fairly sure how Ryan would receive her next piece of news. Sometimes she thought she knew him better than she knew herself.

"Okay, I'll stop you at one bite." He leaned back and crossed his arms over his chest. "Now, what gives? You've got that look."

"What look?"

"That I've-got-a-plan look."

"I do, in fact, have a plan." Phoebe operated with plans. She'd had her fill of surprises and changes when her parents upended her world when she'd been only six. She liked plans. In accordance with her long-term plan, she'd devoted her twenties to building her career.

Right on schedule, she'd realized a major career goal. Now it was time to work on her personal life. "Having a plan isn't a crime."

"Let's hear it. What is it now? Vice presidency within two years?"

"Well, there is that, but this is a little more personal."

"You're going to start yoga classes?"

"No. But maybe that's something to consider." No easy approach to the subject presented itself. "I want to check out Hot Sands as a potential honeymoon site. Elliott and I have been dating for almost a year. Once he makes tenure, we should consider getting engaged."

"Engaged? Honeymoon?" Ryan choked the words out. She'd expected surprise. He looked positively stunned.

"Do you need me to Heimlich you?" Why did she feel so guilty? As if she'd somehow betrayed Ryan?

"You'd really marry *him?*"

"Don't you like Elliott?" Well, that was a stupid question. Since her first prom date at eighteen—no, actually since her first crush on Gary Pelham in middle school—Ryan had always found her boyfriends lacking for one reason or another. Of course, she couldn't say she'd cared much for the girlfriends who flitted in and out of Ryan's life, either.

"He's okay. But not to ma-marry." Ryan stumbled over the word. "Why do you need a husband?" He appeared genuinely perplexed and sounded close to desperation.

"I don't *need* a husband. I *want* a husband. You and I

just turned thirty this year. I want to grow old with someone."

"Remember when we pricked our thumbs and took a blood oath when we were nine? We promised we'd always be friends. *We'll* grow old together. Look. We passed thirty. We're already getting old."

Phoebe studied his earnest expression across the table. Could she make him understand this void in her heart that ached to be filled, the desire for the one thing always denied her? "Not like that. I want a family."

"But you've got your aunt Caroline and uncle Frank."

"Yes. And they're wonderful, but they've been my family on sufferance." She held up a hand to stem his protest. "Loving sufferance, but sufferance nonetheless. They graciously stepped up to the plate when my parents dumped me on them, but we aren't a family by choice. We're a family by obligation. My parents...there's nothing left to say there. I want to build my own family."

"We're like family," he stubbornly maintained.

Ryan's entire life was built around the short term. He leased his sports cars, trading them in for a new model every few years. His sales career brought new faces and new conquests on a daily basis. His girlfriends...well, they'd covered that. The only permanent, long-term fixture in Ryan's life was Phoebe.

She bought her cars and drove them past the point they were paid for. Her job required months on long-term projects. She'd worked with Capshaw and Griffen since she graduated college. For all that Ryan knew her better than anyone else, he didn't seem to understand her craving for stability and a family to call her own.

"Yes. We are like family." Phoebe's connection to Ryan ran soul deep, but she wanted more than friendship. "But I want a ring on my finger that symbolizes commitment. I want a husband to come home to every night, and in a few years a baby. I want the family I've never had.

Naomi plopped down a baklava between them and stopped to finger the Hot Sands brochure. "That looks like a good time. You two going?" She glanced from one to the other.

Ryan sighed. "Phoebe thinks it has honeymoon potential."

Naomi clutched at her blouse. "I feel faint. You two have been coming here once a week for what? Seven, eight years? Every Thursday at twelve-thirty? Finally. Finally the two of you are getting together."

Phoebe tamped down an odd flutter at Naomi's comment. Naomi wasn't the first person over the years to speculate that she and Ryan felt more than friendship for one another. But they were wrong. "Pull yourself out of that faint, Naomi. We're just friends."

Ryan swallowed hard and pasted on a smile. "I'm helping her check out Hot Sands for a honeymoon with another guy. What else are best friends for?"

JUGGLING WONTON SOUP, beef with broccoli, dragon chicken and a six-pack of beer, Ryan knocked on

Phoebe's door. He figured he might as well kill two birds with one stone. They could catch the hockey game on TV and he could try to talk some sense into Phoebe about this crazy marriage thing.

The bitter cold wind sliced through his jacket. Jamaica couldn't come too soon. He hoped Phoebe would come to her senses before they left so he could enjoy his week of sun, sand and sex—and not necessarily in that order.

He knocked on the door again.

"Hold on." Locks turned on the other side, then Phoebe threw the door open. She wore her usual Sunday afternoon attire, old sweats, fuzzy socks and a baggy T-shirt. His shirt, in fact. His T-shirts had a funny way of winding up in Phoebe's closet. "Hey, you. What'd you bring? I'm starving."

"Chinese." He hefted the cartons.

"Good deal." She stepped aside and reached for the six-pack of beer. "Come on in. I'll get this in the fridge. You can put the food on the coffee table."

Ryan placed the cartons on the newspaper-littered coffee table. He shook his head at the mess and smiled. For all that she was the queen of efficiency at work, Phoebes was something of a slob at home. He tossed his jacket on top of hers in the armchair.

While she rounded up paper plates in the kitchen, he flicked on the TV and opened the cartons of steaming food. A fire crackled in the fireplace. Phoebe's place always felt comfortable.

"You want a beer now?" she called from the kitchen.
"Sure."

Bridgette, Phoebe's pound-rescued border collie, ambled over and laid her head against his leg. "Hey, girl. You're not fooling me. I'm old news. It's the take-out you're interested in." She regarded him with solemn brown eyes. "Forget it. This isn't good for dogs."

Phoebe padded in, balancing plates, napkins, silverware and two beers. Her easy laughter washed over him like the familiar waters of a cool stream. "Watch it. She doesn't know she's a d-o-g." Bridgette settled on the floor between the couch and the coffee table.

"She's smart. I think she may have figured it out." He settled on his end of the worn sofa. Phoebe sprawled on the other end, helping herself to the wonton soup. Ryan dished up some dragon chicken. "What're you doing with Bridgette while we're in Jamaica?"

The dog who didn't know she was a dog lifted her black and white head off her paws at the mention of her name.

"Aunt Caroline and Uncle Frank are keeping her. They can't say no to strays." A hint of melancholy tinged her smile and flip comment.

"I don't think they consider it a hardship to care for things they love." His sweet Phoebe—would she ever realize how much Frank and Caroline loved her for herself? "Bridgette'll be happier with them than in a kennel."

"That's what I thought, too." Phoebe turned to the TV. "Now are we gonna watch the game or not?"

"Five bucks says the Rangers take the Flyers." They always bet on the games.

"Point and half, and you're on."

Throughout the first period, Ryan enjoyed Phoebe's animation more than the game. Give her a bit of competition and she positively glowed.

"Did you see that? Did you see that move? He should've whacked that guy." She was a bona fide hockey nut and bloodthirsty as hell. Her sherry-brown eyes sparkled with outrage. Her blond hair stood on end where she'd raked her hand through it.

Ryan laughed. "You're a scary woman."

"Yeah, well, don't forget it." She rolled her eyes at him and went back to the TV.

He was on the verge of bringing up Elliott when she spoke. "So, Keely's all set for Jamaica?"

Damn. It was uncanny how she precipitated him in changing the subject sometimes. "Kiki. Her name is Kiki. And yeah, she's psyched about the trip."

"So what does Kiki do for a living?" she asked without looking away from the game.

"She's a rocket scientist." He dropped the info casually and sat back to enjoy her reaction.

"Yeah. Right. What does she really do?" Phoebe scooped up a piece of broccoli and popped it in her mouth.

"She really is a rocket scientist. Degree in quantum physics." He hadn't known that when he met her at the car wash—only that she was hot with a capital *H*. He hadn't known until he'd bothered to ask last night when they went out.

"You're not kidding?" The absolute shock on Phoebe's face was priceless.

"Degree from MIT and she speaks five languages fluently." He didn't particularly care. He wasn't looking for a long-term relationship, and Kiki was fun with or without her job description, but it seemed to impress the hell out of Phoebe.

"Oh."

Ryan shrugged. "I guess there's at least one smart woman willing to date me, after all." Her comment at Thursday's lunch had crawled under his skin.

Phoebe narrowed her eyes. "What's she look like?"

"Former Miss Texas."

"Oh." Phoebe sat a little straighter on the couch. "Well, then, I can't wait to meet her."

"She's looking forward to meeting you, too."

Phoebe glanced at her T-shirt—technically his T-shirt—and her sweats. "Uh-huh."

"You clean up okay."

"Thanks. I think."

"I'm just teasing. I think you look great just the way you are now." With her soft, messy hair and wearing his shirt, she had a tousled, morning-after look that suddenly struck him as inappropriately, inordinately appealing.

He reached across the space separating them and brushed plum sauce off her lower lip with his thumb, lingering far longer than necessary while a slow heat spiraled through him. "Kind of sexy."

She stared at him as if he'd lost his mind. It was a distinct possibility. He yanked his hand back, disturbed by his reaction to her. This was Phoebe, after all.

Something flashed in her eyes. Caution? Awareness? In an instant it was gone.

"Right." She diffused the tension between them with her flip dismissal, yanking them to the safe path of friendship. "There's plenty of beef and broccoli, if you want some."

"Sure." He plopped a spoonful on his plate to cover the awkwardness he'd introduced. He'd meant to pay her a compliment and wound up damn near making a pass at her. "So, Elliott doesn't mind if Kiki and I come along on the trip?"

Phoebe shrugged, "He was distracted but fine with it when I talked to him on the phone."

"Have you thought through this potential thing—" he couldn't bring himself to say marriage "—with Elliott?"

"Of course I have. I'm fond of him. We get along well together. He's stable. Dependable. I think it's a good plan." The obstinate tilt of her chin echoed her defiant words.

Crap. If he didn't do something, Phoebe'd wind up married to Elliott just for the sake of seeing her damn plan through to fruition. And Elliott was all wrong for Phoebe because...hell, Ryan didn't exactly know why, he just knew Elliott was.

If Phoebe really had her heart set on a husband, Ryan would help her find one. Later. Maybe when they returned from Jamaica. Someone who appreciated her beauty and wit and her multitude of good qualities, but not so wimpy he couldn't stand up to her strong, take-charge personality and fierce competitive streak. That someone wasn't Elliott.

Ryan sighed silently into his beer. He'd have to figure out a way to convince her, because friends didn't let friends marry the wrong person.

2

"WELCOME!"

Phoebe smiled at the young man who greeted her and Ryan at the restaurant entrance.

"Two?"

"Four. We're expecting two more."

"Certainly. If you will come with me, please."

They followed him along the covered walkway to the dining area. Of all the resort brochures Phoebe had looked over, the resort's smaller, intimate size and this restaurant had sold her on Hot Sands. The open-air restaurant, supported by stone pilings and covered by a thatched roof, jettisoned over the sparkling aquamarine waters of the Caribbean.

They wound past a number of tables until the maître d' stopped beside a round one next to the rail, overlooking the translucent blue-green water.

"How is this?" He pulled out a fan-backed rattan chair.

"It's perfect." Enchanted, Phoebe sank into the cushioned seat.

"Your waiter will be with you in a moment."

"We'll hold off until the other two arrive," Ryan said, taking his seat next to her.

Phoebe sighed with pure pleasure as she looked around and absorbed everything. Straight ahead and to her right the calm expanse of water, a kaleidoscope of tranquil blues, continued until it reached the sky. A smattering of white clouds floated above the horizon.

To her left, a pristine sugar-sand beach stretched along the shoreline, bordered by lush, tropical jungle and windswept palms. She glanced over her shoulder, past the restaurant and the colonial Spanish architecture of the resort, to the faraway rise of the verdant Blue Mountains, home of some of the best coffee in the world.

Shouts from a distant beach volleyball game underscored the rhythm of calypso piped in over discreetly placed speakers. The gentle lapping of the sea against the rocks drifted up from the pilings and mingled with the murmur of conversation from other tables.

A warm Jamaican breeze shifted against her skin, carrying with it a mixture of salt air, coconut oil and Ryan's familiar scent. Overhead ceiling fans lazily stirred the thick, tropical air into an exotic blend. Utter contentment stole through her.

Impulsively, she reached for Ryan's hand. "Isn't it beautiful? I'm so glad you're here." It wouldn't be the same if she couldn't share this perfect place with him.

Phoebe wound her fingers through his. Surely her heightened senses led her to imagine the fleeting shock when his fingers curled around hers.

Ryan's green eyes held a slightly bemused expression. "The brochures don't do it justice." His fingers tightened around hers. "Everything's brighter. Bolder. You can't feel that breeze in a brochure, can you?"

The warm wind slid over her skin. "That's exactly how I feel—more vibrant and alive." That explained the irrational leap of her pulse earlier. "This is a perfect honeymoon spot."

An image popped into her mind. She was wearing a simple white dress with her veil blowing in the breeze and the shift of fine powdery sand beneath her bare feet, feeling the steady clasp of her new husband's hand in hers and seeing the heated promise in his green eyes.... Urk. Her fantasy ground to a halt.

What was Ryan doing in her fantasy? Elliott belonged there. She took a deep breath to calm her racing heart. No harm done. Just a little brain spasm brought on by the beautiful setting and Ryan's proximity. Absolutely nothing more.

She freed her hand on the pretext of lifting her hair off her neck. Now seemed like a good time to focus on Ryan's near-perfect date. "When will Kiki be down?"

Ryan shrugged. "She was on the phone checking on a project. She wasn't sure how long it would take. What do you think of her?"

Phoebe rearranged her napkin on the white linen table cloth. "You've hit the jackpot." Which proved the old adage, be careful what you wish for because you might get it. She'd worried that Ryan would continue to flit from relationship to relationship. So why did she feel disconcerted by Kiki's near perfection? An insidious voice inside her head whispered to her. *Because*

*she's the first woman you feel threatened by. Because you can
see her displacing you in Ryan's life.* "She could be the
one."

"The one?" Ryan stared at her as if Phoebe had spoken in tongues.

"You know, the one you can't resist. The one who
breaks your heart." *She should be very happy for him.*
"She's beautiful. Great body. Brains out the wazoo. A
degree in quantum physics. Speaks five languages fluently, three of which are dead. I think that about covers
it."

"I'm glad you like her."

Phoebe thought it best not to correct him. She *should*
like Kiki. There was no reason not to. Twofold guilt ate
at her. First, she'd imagined herself on a honeymoon
with Ryan, the woman's date. And second, she
couldn't quite get past a niggling dislike of the other
woman. Guilt urged her on.

"I feel like a flat-chested Amazon next to her. I'm at
least a head taller and a cup size smaller than she is.
And she has beautiful orthodontia, as well." Phoebe
ran her tongue along the small gap between her two
slightly crooked front teeth. She'd grown boobs since
high school, but nothing of Kiki's magnitude.

Ryan laughed and took stock of her while she
groused. His gaze swept over the bodice of her sarong-
style dress and up. Laughter died in the back of his
throat. His eyes darkened.

"There's nothing wrong with your orthodontia." His
gaze dropped to her breasts. "Or the rest of you."

A shiver chased across her skin. Something danger-ously akin to sexual attraction blossomed inside her, a woman's response to a man's appreciative look. Except she was the woman and her best friend was the man and there was no room for looks and responses like that between them.

Confusion filled her. "Ryan—"

"Hi, guys." Kiki slid into a chair next to Ryan.

Phoebe blinked. The tension binding them disap-peared like an ephemeral whiff of smoke gusted by a strong wind. Had she imagined the last minute? There was something about this place. She'd make sure she didn't fall prey to further flights of fancy about Ryan.

"Sorry I took so long," Kiki apologized, stunning in a short jungle print dress that showcased her curves to full advantage. Her dark hair was twisted into a so-phisticated chignon.

Strands of hair clung to Phoebe's sweat-dampened neck. Kiki looked fresh and chic and sexy. Phoebe felt rumpled and sweaty in comparison.

"Not a problem. We were just enjoying the spectac-ular view." Ryan nodded toward the expanse of beach, ocean and sky. "Everything okay at work?"

Kiki ignored the view. "They're managing without me. Barely. It's amazing the level of people the space program settles for these days. I'll need to check in every evening before the west coast office closes." She eyed the empty seat at their table, a near predatory look sharpening her features. "Where's Elliott?"

Elliott and Kiki had gotten along like the proverbial

house on fire during the two-hour ride from the airport to the resort. Both had completed undergraduate work at Loyola. And it turned out that Kiki occasionally visited Vanderbilt as a guest lecturer.

"He wanted to unpack before he came down. He should be here in a few minutes," Phoebe said. She bit back disappointment that Elliott had shown more eagerness to put away his underwear than explore the resort.

"I unpacked while I was on the phone." Kiki nodded as if she completely understood Elliott's compulsion. She looked past Phoebe. "Here's Elliott now." She turned on a sixty-watt smile. "We were just talking about you," Kiki said, welcoming him.

"Sorry I took so long." Elliott dropped into the empty seat between Phoebe, and Kiki, a lock of dark hair hanging over his forehead, his dark eyes brooding. Phoebe and Elliott had both been busy with work. Aside from a snatched lunch one afternoon, they hadn't seen one another for a few weeks. But now that the right man had arrived, Phoebe was ready for some island magic.

"You're here now, and that's all that matters." She leaned forward and pressed her lips to his lean cheek, eager to embrace the magic. No shiver. No quiver. No magic.

Phoebe sat back, nonplussed.

"All unpacked and settled in?" Ryan asked. His smile wore a faint edge of sarcasm.

Elliott frowned. "Almost. I ordered extra towels and

pillows from room service." He twined his fingers through Phoebe's, his touch cool and antiseptic. "How about a drink to celebrate being here?" He glanced around expectantly.

As if on cue, a waiter appeared. "Hello. I am Martin. I will be your waiter." His lilting accent brought a smile to Phoebe's face. "You have just arrived in Jamaica today?"

Ryan laughed, "How can you tell?"

"You do not yet have the sun-kissed look of relaxation." Martin returned a ready smile. Maybe that was it. She needed sun-kissed relaxation. "Perhaps I can bring something to drink? Our house specialty is made with a local rum, which is most excellent."

"And what exactly is in that drink other than rum?" Elliott asked.

"We begin with pineapple juice and blend it with coconut milk, some of our local rum and a touch of grenadine. It is a favorite among guests. Quite potent."

Elliott and Kiki both ordered the house special.

Although it sounded yummy, rum left her with a headache, and she wanted to savor ever moment of this vacation. Phoebe opted for a ginger beer, and Ryan ordered a Red Stripe lager.

"Very good. I will return shortly with your drinks." Martin hurried away.

Phoebe picked up her menu, aware that breakfast had been a quick piece of toast several hours ago. "I'm ravenous."

Casual conversation floated around the table as

everyone looked over the menu. Within minutes Martin arrived, dispensing their drinks with a flourish.

"Very good. Might I suggest a *boonoonoonoos* platter for lunch? It is a sampler of our local dishes, an excellent introduction to Jamaican food."

"Let's have that," Phoebe said, eager to try the local cuisine.

Elliott turned up his nose. "No, thanks, I'll have a turkey sandwich, shaved not sliced, on whole wheat. Light mayo. Lettuce and tomato on the side."

"The last thing I want to do is come to a foreign country and get sick eating the local food. I'll have a turkey sandwich, as well," Kiki instructed Martin.

Phoebe shuddered at Kiki's rude comment. Despite the relaxed, open-air structure, they were dining at a four-star resort, not eating from a street vendor's food stall.

Ryan caught Phoebe's eye and shook his head, reading her indignation as clearly as if she'd voiced it. "We'll try the sampler platter."

Martin left, their orders in hand.

Phoebe tasted her drink, inhaling the fragrant aroma of ginger, savoring its cool, refreshing bite against her tongue. "Delicious."

Determined to tap into the island's underlying sensuality with the appropriate person—her date—Phoebe ran her fingers along Elliott's forearm. The only thing she felt was the soft smattering of dark hair beneath her fingertips. "How's the house special?"

He pursed his lips—sculpted, full, Phoebe had

thought his mouth sexy from the first time she'd seen him—and considered his drink. "A touch more coconut milk, and it'd be superb."

Martin arrived with their food. "How are your drinks? Is everyone enjoying?" He placed a steaming platter, fragrant with exotic spices, between Phoebe and Ryan and served Elliott and Kiki turkey sandwiches prepared to Elliott's exacting specifications. "Is there anything else you desire?"

"Fresh ground pepper on my turkey. Please," Elliott said.

Phoebe brushed aside a flicker of annoyance. Elliott knew what he liked and liked what he knew. She should view it as an asset, a measure of his stability.

Having peppered Elliott's sandwich, Martin gestured toward the food on the table. "Enjoy. You may want to take a siesta after this. We have a saying in Jamaica. The days are long, but the nights are longer." Martin retreated with a good-humored laugh.

A siesta. A few hours in the cool, quiet intimacy of their room. Perhaps a relaxing hour in their private pool or a soak in the whirlpool tub in their sumptuous marbled bathroom. The idea left her flat. Here she was in one of the most sensuous, romantic places on earth with a handsome man, and the strongest emotion she felt toward him at this point was annoyance.

Ryan shifted in the seat beside her, his hair-roughened knee brushing against her leg. The brief contact sizzled up her thigh. She jerked her leg away.

Ryan appeared mercifully oblivious to her errant hormonal reactions.

Something was terribly amiss. Elliott's touch left her cold, while Ryan's sizzled through her. Maybe she'd suffered some weird form of jet lag, although Nashville and Ocho Rios were in the same time zone. Or maybe she desperately needed that siesta to get her head screwed on straight.

Determined to put her inappropriate responses to the two men at the table behind her, Phoebe spooned a sampling from each dish, her mouth watering from the exotic aromas. "I spent too many hours this month behind a desk. This weather's fantastic. Let's make a plan for this afternoon."

Kiki caught her enthusiasm. "What about Jet Skis? We should be able to get a few hours in." Kiki nodded toward two couples on machines racing across the blue-green water in the distance.

Ryan nodded, his green eyes alight, always ready for fun. "It'll be a blast. What do you think?"

He looked from Phoebe to Elliott.

"Sounds good to me. It was one of the things I wanted to try while we were here," Phoebe said.

"You've never been on a Jet Ski before?" Did Phoebe imagine that note of condescension in Kiki's question?

"Neither have I," Elliott confessed.

"Oh, my. Two Jet Ski virgins," Kiki drawled. She arched her brows at Ryan. "Did you know we had two virgins here? We'll definitely have to initiate them into the pleasures of wave riding, won't we?"

Kiki's heavy innuendo mingled with the exotic spices permeating the air.

Ryan's mouth quirked in a smile. "Phoebe, you could ride with me—"

"And I'd consider it an honor to initiate Elliott," Kiki interrupted.

"Only if you promise to be gentle with me," Elliott protested with mock innocence.

Elliott had a sense of humor? He'd never displayed even a hint of playfulness with Phoebe.

"Trust me, it'll be so good, you'll beg for another ride," Kiki promised, skimming one of her long red nails down his arm.

"How can I turn down an offer like that?" Elliott capitulated.

"What do you think, Phoebe?" Kiki asked.

She thought she could vamp with the best of them, that's what she thought. Kiki had Elliott all but drooling in his turkey sandwich. Phoebe glanced at Ryan from beneath her lashes, "I can't think of anyone I'd rather be with my first time."

His eyes held hers. "I promise you'll enjoy it."

A slow flush ran over her, through her. "You don't think my inexperience is a problem?"

"All you have to do is hold on and leave the rest to me. I'll make it good for you. I've had lots of practice."

She didn't doubt it for a minute.

PHOEBE DREW the drapes over the French doors, plunging the room into cool shadows. The glazed tile floor was warm beneath her bare feet where the midafternoon sun had slanted in. As she retreated into the room and approached the four-poster bed, the tiles grew cooler against her soles.

She wrapped one arm around the wooden post of the footboard and leaned into it. Elliott presented a spectacular specimen of manhood stretched out on the bed. How appropriate he taught classical Greek and Roman literature. He possessed striking, classical looks. Aquiline nose. Chiseled lips. Hooded eyes with a sweep of dark lashes. At five feet nine inches, she was no shrinking violet, yet he topped her by several inches. His legs, while not particularly muscular, were long and lean.

"You need to grade *all* those papers?"

He glanced up from the stack before him. "Uh-huh. I should be finished in a couple of hours. In time for Jet Skiing."

Instead of disappointment, relief washed over her. They'd drifted farther apart in the last few weeks than she realized. They needed a little more time together before she was ready to climb into a whirlpool tub with him.

Tonight, they'd enjoy a few glasses of wine over a romantic dinner—how could it be anything less in Jamaica—and things would feel different between them.

And what about Ryan and Kiki? She bet no one was grading papers in their room. How many girlfriends had Ryan run through in the course of their friendship? She'd lost count long ago. So, what chemical imbalance in her brain rendered the prospect of Kiki and Ryan together bothersome now?

Phoebe shoved away from the bed. She'd find something to do other than watch Elliott immerse himself in paperwork and speculate on Ryan and Kiki's sexcapades. They'd arranged to meet at the Jet Ski dock. She'd be there.

In the meantime, there were things to do. Places to explore. Phoebe slid her feet into a pair of sandals. "I'll see you at four."

"Hmm," Elliott murmured, engrossed.

She slipped out of the room. She doubted Elliott even knew she'd left. A restless energy propelled her along the walkway skirting the lush, barely contained jungle garden. She paused, transfixed by color-splashed parrots perched in the dense foliage.

"They are beautiful, yes?" Startled, Phoebe looked around to find their lunch waiter, Martin.

"Yes. They are beautiful. Everything here is." Martin wasn't wearing his white waiter's jacket. "Are you through for the day?"

"It is my break before the dinner hour begins. I will bicycle home to see my wife and children. It is only six miles from the resort."

Twelve miles round-trip to see his family, before returning for another shift? "How many children do you have?"

"A boy and a girl. Seven and five. They are most excellent children. Very smart. They must go to bed early for school. They are asleep when I finish with the dinner hour." He pulled a worn photo from his back pocket.

A boy and a girl, wearing school uniforms and Martin's smile, flanked a tall, slender woman with long braids and kind, laughing eyes. The three stood before a sun-yellow cinder-block house. "They're lovely. They look like you. That's your wife?"

"Yes. Mathilda." He pointed to the boy and girl. "Terrence and Louise. I am a very rich man."

The light in Martin's eyes brought tears to hers. They both knew he didn't refer to material wealth. His obvious devotion to his family intensified her resolve to have the same. "Yes. I think you are a very rich man. Thank you for sharing your family with me."

He tucked the photo into his pocket. "You do not wish to have a siesta?"

"I think I'm too excited to siesta." It sounded better than, *My boyfriend is busy grading papers and I'm in a green-eyed sulk because my best friend is cozying up with Kiki.*

"Perhaps you have a bit of the native in you." He tilted his head to one side and considered her. "I hope you do not find me forward, but have you ever thought to wear braids?"

"Like Mathilda's? No. I never thought about it."

"You possess lovely bones of the face. It would be a most excellent choice for you. If you decide to try this, go to the salon here at Hot Sands. Ask for Katrina. She is my cousin and the best braider in Ocho Rios. Tell her

Martin has sent you. She will do quite an excellent job for you. I think you will be most pleased."

No one had ever mentioned before that she possessed lovely bones. Martin probably received a nice fat kickback from Cousin Katrina for any business he sent her way, but Phoebe couldn't possibly begrudge anything to a man so enamored of his family.

A head full of braids struck her as just the thing to do. And it would look sexy, to boot. Perhaps her problem wasn't Elliott as much as it was her attitude. Braids offered a more sophisticated, sleek alternative to a ponytail or having hair cling to her sweaty neck.

"Thank you, Martin. I'll look Katrina up right now. Enjoy your family."

"That I will. I look forward to serving you during the dinner hour."

3

RYAN CHECKED his watch. Again. He'd made it his personal philosophy to never worry, but worry niggled at him. And it was Phoebe's fault. While Kiki lived by the fashionably late code—she'd nearly missed the flight this morning—punctuality almost qualified as a religious principle for Phoebe.

She was officially thirteen minutes late meeting them at the pier. Elliott, who said he'd been grading papers, was clueless as to her whereabouts. How could Phoebe, who had so much going for her, possibly consider tying herself to this guy until death—or, more likely, divorce—they did part?

Nothing had happened between him and Kiki, but they hadn't been dating for ten months, either. Kiki had sequestered herself in the bathroom for a facial and a pedicure.

He'd spent his time trying to get Phoebe's flirtatious teasing out of his head. *I can't think of anyone I'd rather be with my first time.* How many times and with how many women had he engaged in the same meaningless innuendo? But never with Phoebe. She'd never slanted her almond-shaped eyes at him in invitation until today. Her voice had never dropped to that husky octave and wrapped around him like a lover's touch. And if he'd had any damn sense, he'd have seduced Kiki during the siesta and forgotten all about Phoebe.

"Check her out," Elliott said.

Ryan glanced up. A sexy, braided blonde strode across the white sand. *Wow*. For a second something struck him as vaguely familiar about that self-confident stride. *Right*. That fell into the wishful thinking category. For the first time, he felt a kinship with Elliott—ill-begotten, lust-ridden admiration for an incredible pair of legs and a sexy swagger.

"You're not kidding." Hell, he could barely breathe. "The braids and those legs that go on forever..." In the span of a heartbeat, his mind had her naked beneath him with those luscious legs wrapped around his waist.

"Actually, I meant Kiki. But, yes, Phoebe's definitely got nice legs."

Phoebe? *Phoebe?* What the— Ryan whipped off his Ray-Bans and squinted against the sun. Hell's bells. No wonder he recognized that walk. Ryan shoved his sunglasses on and belatedly noticed Kiki next to Phoebe.

The women passed a beach volleyball game. A guy playing front net position turned to gawk at them, his mouth hanging open. A spiked ball caught him square in the back, throwing him to the sand. Served the clown right.

"Sorry we're late." Kiki linked her arm through his. "Kiki and I ran into one another on the way out."

Phoebe smoothed a hand over her head. "So, what do you guys think?"

Beaded cornrows brushed her shoulders, the style accentuating her high cheekbones and the fullness of her mouth. A thin white cotton T-shirt offered a teasing glimpse of her bikini. Since they'd arrived in Jamaica, he'd noticed all kinds of new things about Phoebe. And he had no business responding with fantasies of her beneath him, that's what he thought.

"It's definitely different." Elliott considered her with his head cocked to one side. "But it suits you."

"Why in the hell did you go and do that?" The minute the words left his mouth he realized he sounded like an ass. He just wasn't used to this sexy, fantasy-inducing version of Phoebe.

"Come on, Ryan, why don't you tell me how you really feel about it?"

Damnation. He'd hurt her feelings. His earlier fantasy flashed through his head. How he really felt about her at this point would scare the hell out of her. It did him. "Sorry, Phoebes, I'm just used to you the other way. It looks great."

"I think it's awesome. Wish I had the bone structure to carry it off," Kiki said with a pout.

Elliott flashed a cavalier smile and eyed her brimming bikini top. "There's nothing wrong with your structure."

Kiki preened, and Phoebe's eyebrows arched above her sunglasses.

Elliott was an idiot, Ryan thought. Why was he flirting with Kiki when he had a gorgeous woman already?

Phoebe planned. Ryan seized opportunity when it stared him in the face. Kiki and Elliott. If the professor kept putting the move on Kiki, Ryan wouldn't have to worry about Phoebe walking down the aisle with Elliott. All Ryan had to do was offer a little subtle encouragement, toss them together and watch the sparks fly. Elliott had never been worthy of Phoebe and was about to prove it. Ryan was more than happy to give Elliott ample rope to hang himself. Of course, this meant he wouldn't be taking things any further with Kiki, but a week of sun and sand without the sex was a small price to pay to keep Phoebe from making the mistake of a lifetime.

Ryan bit back a smirk and tossed a Jet Ski key to Kiki. "You and Elliott take number twenty-seven. We'll take twenty-eight."

Kiki eagerly mounted the Jet Ski and beckoned to Elliott. "I haven't had a virgin in a very long time."

Elliott climbed on behind and wrapped his arms around her middle. Given their height difference, Elliot's hands hovered just below Kiki's breasts. Kiki revved her engine.

The steady ocean breeze stirred up a potent mixture of suntan lotion and the fragrance Phoebe favored. What was it with Phoebe today? Was it the allure of the unknown in what he'd always considered a known quantity that had his heart pounding like a teenager on a first date? Once he got used to her new look, he'd be back to normal.

"I'd say Elliott's about one wave away from copping a feel," Phoebe muttered with more than a touch of asperity in Ryan's ear. Her arm pressed against his waist, wreaking havoc with his composure.

Kiki called, "We're out of here. Catch up with us."

Ryan waved her on. "I think you're right about that feel. Elliott's enjoying sitting behind her. And Kiki doesn't seem to mind."

"Do *you* mind?"

"No. I needed a woman to vacation at a couples-only resort. There's nothing between us except a few fun dates." And that's all it'd ever be, because he'd be damned if he'd sit back and watch Phoebe make a huge mistake with Elliott. He knew what Phoebe was like once she decided on a plan.

"Teach me how to drive this thing." Phoebe's lips quirked to one side, her gearing-up-to-kick-butt expression. "I'm going to run circles around Kiki." She gathered her braids together and secured them behind her head. "Okay?"

Damn. Therein lay the downside to seizing opportunities without thinking them through. The last thing he wanted was Phoebe in a head-to-head competition for Elliott. But if he, Ryan, distracted her with a little light flirtation along the lines of lunch today... Hell, that was what he did best. He'd just never done it with Phoebe. He could handle it, and in the end, if it kept Phoebe from marrying Elliott, it was worth it.

"I don't know about you driving, Phoebes. This being your first time and everything." He struck just the right chord with that teasing note, not too suggestive.

Phoebe dug a bottle of sunscreen out of her bag. "Can you get the middle of my back? Elliott was already gone, and I couldn't reach it myself." She tugged her T-shirt off. "I don't want to get burned my first time." She extended the bottle with a sassy smile, "Actually, I don't want to get burned at all."

He stood transfixed. Heaven help him. All over the beach, women wore much briefer, much more revealing bikinis, but none wore them as well as Phoebe. A slow heat burned low in his belly and spiraled through him.

"Ryan?" She waved the suncreen in front of his face. "Are you going to help me out here or do you want me to ask that guy playing volleyball?"

He snatched the bottle. She wasn't about to ask the guy who'd been gaping at her. "Turn around."

She presented her back to him. He'd always appreciated the feminine lines of a woman's back. Phoebe's took his breath away—the graceful curve leading to the flare of her hips, the slight hollow of her spine. Ryan poured a generous amount of lotion into one hand and passed her the bottle over her shoulder. He rubbed his unsteady hands together. *Get a grip, man. This is Phoebe. Slap on the lotion and be done with it.*

The instant his hands touched her shoulders, he realized he'd severely underestimated the task at hand. His palms, slicked with the warm lotion, glided over the supple silk of her sun-heated skin. That hiss of indrawn breath belonged to him.

His hands and fingertips took on a mind of their own, stroking and massaging her pliant flesh. Which was a good thing, considering his brain damn near ceased functioning, content to relish the fine texture of her skin, the sensual line of her back, her scent.

He splayed his fingers under her bikini strap. She quivered beneath his palm, and a response echoed through him. Careful not to leave any skin untouched, he smoothed the lotion down her spine to the small of her back. Another quiver radiated from her to him. She was so sensitive, so arousingly responsive to his touch, and his hand had only stroked her back.

Ryan quelled an insane urge to slip his hands beneath the elastic of her bottoms and massage the fullness of her bare buttocks. He'd whisper sweet words in her ear until she willingly sought a secluded section of beach and indulged his earlier fantasy. Perhaps if it had been any other woman, but this was Phoebe.

All she'd asked him to do was put sunscreen on her back, not work himself into some delusional state.

He dropped his hands to his sides and reminded himself she was his friend. *Think friend, not woman,* he instructed his libido, his brain and all the other body parts that suddenly seemed to have minds of their own.

She turned. "I'm ready. I don't want to be a virgin anymore."

His body blatantly ignored his instruction.

PHOEBE CHECKED her watch. Eleven o'clock. After the flight down, the exhilaration of skimming over the turquoise sea with Ryan and the lively discussion over one of the finest dinners she'd ever enjoyed, she ought to be exhausted. Instead she was energized. Restless. Eager.

Despite the hour, the night felt young and brimming with life. In the nearby garden, birds called to one another. The night air carried the perfume of foreign blooms and exotic spices, borne by the ocean breeze. The low murmur of lovers whispered beneath the strident tones of partygoers.

Around the curve of the winding walkway, rawly sensual Caribbean music pulsed from the Jungle Room. Phoebe slid her arm around Elliott's waist, her hips instinctively responding to the music's rhythm. Caught up in the moment, she looked at Ryan and Kiki. "Come on. Let's go dance."

Kiki grabbed Ryan's hand and tugged him along. "I love to dance."

"Then let's find the Jungle Room."

Elliott, with three generous glasses of wine under his belt from dinner, displayed more enthusiasm than aptitude as he swayed down the torch-lined walkway. "Bring on the limbo."

Phoebe laughed with the sheer exuberance of the night.

"I didn't know you liked to dance, Phoebe," Ryan commented as he and Kiki followed them.

Phoebe had realized earlier in the day that, as well as

she and Ryan knew one another, there was a whole layer beneath the surface neither knew. While they'd discussed their other relationships over the years, they'd steadfastly avoided any recognition of one another's sensuality. When Ryan had smoothed on suntan lotion, she'd discovered a whole new side to him. And to herself. His touch had turned her inside out.

"Maybe there's a thing or two about me that you don't know." She tossed the words over her shoulder. Try as she might to keep her tone light, a hint of provocation crept in.

"How long have you two been friends?" Kiki asked.

"Twenty-four years," Phoebe said. The music grew louder as they got closer to the club.

"Don't you ever get tired of one another?"

Ryan was one of the most interesting people she knew. "No."

"No."

They answered simultaneously.

Elliott tightened his arm about Phoebe's shoulders, pulling her closer to his side. "She might not get tired of him, but I do. He's around all the damn time," Elliott groused to no one in particular. "No offense, Ryan."

"None taken." Ryan laughed off Elliott's comment.

"Twenty-four years and you've never..."

"No," Phoebe reassured her, not that Kiki seemed insecure, just curious as if their relationship presented an oddity to be dissected. And maybe on another night in another place, Phoebe might have been offended by her curiosity and her questions. But not here and now.

The heat of the night and rhythm of the music invited lascivious thoughts.

Kiki stopped within a few feet of the club doorway. "Come on. Twenty-four years and neither one of you ever even thought about it? I'm not buying it."

She'd wondered once or twice on occasion. And since they'd arrived at the island, she'd felt the under-current, the subtle flirtation between them, but it wouldn't go any further. Phoebe wasn't willing to share that just to satisfy Kiki's curiosity. She shook her head, laughing at Kiki's insistence.

Elliott waved his hand in the air. "Believe it. They're like brother and sister."

In the flickering torchlight, Phoebe glanced at Ryan. Her breath caught in her throat and her blood raced. She was caught up in the spell of calypso and the look in his eyes that acknowledged he'd thought about her too.

Yes, she'd wondered. And now she knew he'd done the same. On a sane, rational day the thought would terrify her. But there was nothing sane or rational about a Caribbean night. Tonight, the thought excited her.

"I think my *sister's* ready to dance."

They stepped into the dimly lit club. The air hung thick with perfume and aftershave, cigarette smoke, a faint whiff of ganja, the cloying sweetness of rum, and sexual arousal. Couples packed the dance floor. The music, loud and rhythmic, entered Phoebe, became one with her body, precluding conversation, ousting inhibitions. It pulsed in her, through her, a fever. Words were extemporaneous. Primal movement reigned—contagious hedonism at its finest.

The four of them surged into the crush of people on the dance floor. Phoebe gave herself over to the music's driving beat. Gyrating. Undulating. Her body responded to the music's demand with seductive movements, the music filling her, compelling her to a place beyond her usual bounds.

Within minutes, the crowd swallowed Kiki and Elliott. Ryan, however, was still there, separated from her by a handful of people. He made his way to her. She leaned close, still dancing, her mouth next to his ear to be heard above the music and noise. "Kiki and Elliott?"

Ryan shrugged and shook his head. His lips were warm against the shell of her ear. "Don't know. Doesn't matter."

His mouth, the heat underlying the laughter in his eyes, his hard body against hers in the crush of the dance floor, the music's relentless throb compelled her. Phoebe snaked her arms around Ryan's neck in invitation, her hips seconding the offer. Laughing, seductive, she retreated. Eyes glittering, he accepted her challenge and followed.

A crowded dance floor offered the opportunity to seduce without consequence. Dancing to the wildly uninhibited music, she crossed a line she'd never consider actually approaching. Dance became mind sex.

Dark sensuality wove between them, bound them.

Advance and retreat. Undulating. Thrusting. Pulsing. Grinding.

In the heat of the music, the night, the moment, it seemed the most natural thing in the world for Ryan to pull her tight against him. Caught up in the erotic rhythms seething between them, Phoebe crossed the line she'd only allowed herself to fantasize about occasionally. She boldly claimed his mouth. Ryan moaned against her lips, his fingers molded against the sweat-slicked skin of her back. Teasing tantalization gave way to fervent fusion. She closed her eyes as he explored her mouth with his tongue. Murmuring deep in her throat, she suckled him. As if a line ran straight to his erection, she felt him pulse against her. Feverish, thick passion flowed through her. Where did her heat end and his begin? She surged against him, burning up with a fire only he could put out.

He wrenched his mouth from hers. "Phoebe?"

Eyes still closed, still on a sensual high, she licked her swollen lips.

"Phoebe?" She opened her eyes. Ryan's green eyes probed hers, a thousand questions rolled into her name.

What had she done? This was her best friend she was grinding against, hot to the point of madness.

"I'm sorry...I shouldn't have—"

And then, having crossed the line to a place from which there was no return, she did what any self-respecting coward would do.

She ran like hell.

4

THE NEXT MORNING Ryan waited for Phoebe by the pool. Over breakfast, Kiki and Elliott had announced plans to play the slot machines in the lounge, both citing hangovers from the night before, which left Ryan and Phoebe to follow through on the canoeing plans they'd made over dinner the previous evening. Ryan also had a hangover, but his had nothing to do with alcohol. Phoebe and her hot kiss had kept him up most of the night.

"Ready?" Phoebe pasted on a bright smile. He read her determination to ignore the previous evening's activities.

"Sure. This way." Ryan started in the general direction of the beach. "The concierge said the canoes are down here and it's just a short distance to the cliffs. It's supposed to be spectacular."

Uncomfortable silence stretched between them.

"Ryan—"

"Phoebe—"

She cut in with a rush of words. "Listen, Ryan, I'm sorry about last night."

"I'm not." He tried to make her feel better.

"You should be. It never should've happened."

"You're probably right." It probably would've been better if he'd never tasted her passion. It had haunted him all night, and even now he craved another taste.

"I wasn't myself. I just got carried away with the wine and the music and the night. You could've been anyone."

"Is that supposed to make me feel better?" That was a royal slap in the ego.

"I just wanted you to understand where I was coming from. Don't let this come between us, because it really didn't mean anything."

"Fine." He didn't much care for being told he had been just a warm body in the right place at the right time.

"Can we just forget about it?"

"I said that's fine, Phoebe. It's forgotten. Done. History."

They reached the canoes lined up at the edge of the water. An attendant offered them a friendly smile. "It's a beautiful morning for canoeing. The water is nice and calm. You will go around this curve and then you will find yourself next to our magnificient Caribbean cliffs." He pointed to a western point on the shoreline. "Choose whichever boat you like."

Ryan and Phoebe selected the first boat, and the attendant handed them each a paddle.

"I haven't been in a canoe since we were out on the lake in high school," Ryan commented.

"That's right, you missed the trip I took last year. You had that sales meeting. You'll remember everything in no time. What'll make it easier for you? Do you want me in the front or behind?" Phoebe asked.

It was a perfectly legitimate question to pose to someone you were getting in a canoe with. Unfortunately, it stirred erotic images of her undulating before him on the dance floor last night.

"Take the front." He managed a nice even tone despite the rush of desire her words unleashed.

Phoebe positioned herself in the bow. Ryan shoved off from the white-sand shore and climbed in. With fluid, graceful movements, she dipped her paddle into the clear blue water and pulled. Her T-shirt hugged the line of her back and the womanly flare of her hips.

Distracted, thrown off, Ryan chopped the water with his paddle.

Phoebe glanced over her shoulder. "Take your time. Remember—long, smooth strokes. Make sure it's in before you pull through."

She demonstrated her long, smooth stroke for him. "See?"

He clearly saw that it was going to be a long, torturous day.

THAT EVENING, by the end of the second course, Kiki and Elliott had drifted into a discussion of the inner workings of Vanderbilt, leaving Ryan and Phoebe to what amounted to an intimate dinner for two.

Ryan studied Phoebe. In the shimmering candlelight, her skin glowed honey gold, and her eyes sparkled like a fine sherry. How many times had he seen her without really seeing her? How had he overlooked her provocative sensuality? All these years, he'd taken her for granted, assuming he knew her, only to discover she had hidden layers and depths he hadn't begun to discern. She was a complex woman he'd reduced to one dimension.

Canoeing with Phoebe had proved a subtle form of torture. The curve of her back as she paddled had teased him. Her scent drifting back on the breeze, the memory of last night's kiss had kept him aroused.

"You're awfully quiet tonight," Phoebe said. She seemed to have effectively forgotten that shatteringly erotic dance and kiss.

"Maybe you wore me out earlier today." Shit, he had no business flirting with Phoebe.

Phoebe's eyebrows arched above the sweep of her lashes. "I think it was probably your extracurricular activities before dinner." Was she fishing for information on him and Kiki?

"The only thing extracurricular in my room was Kiki's two-hour preparations. There were exhausting to watch." Kiki defined high maintenance. "Have some mango brulee." He nudged the dish toward her. He'd ordered it for her, anyway.

She picked up her spoon. "Maybe just a bite."

Ryan grinned and shook his head. Phoebe and her parceled bites of pleasure. She raised a spoonful of the dessert to her mouth, her lashes lowering in anticipation. She opened her mouth and slipped the spoon inside, wrapping her lips around it. "Mmm." She opened her eyes as she slid the spoon out.

How many times had he seen her do the very same thing? Savor a bite with deliberation. But never, until now, with such a devastating effect. Ryan damn near choked as his brain supplied a visual of something other than a spoon sliding between her lips. He tried to will away the image. "Good?"

She shook her head, the beads in the ends of her hair brushing against her bared shoulders. "Better than good." Her brown eyes glimmered with sublime pleasure. "Orgasmic."

She'd said it before. This time, though, the word sizzled into his brain, tightened his groin. He reached for his water glass and took a long, cold drink. It didn't do any good.

She dipped her spoon in the dish. "You've got to try this." She leaned forward, proffering her spoon.

"No, thanks."

"You should at least try it." She teased the spoon in his direction, and the neckline of her halter top shifted, offering Ryan a glimpse of succulent golden skin. "Isn't your mouth watering for a bite?"

She was killing him. Hell, yes, his mouth was watering. He leaned slightly forward and then caught himself. He deliberately looked away. "No, thanks."

"Come on. Aren't you even tempted? You're always willing to try something new." Her voice was low and husky, and he wasn't sure if the note of seduction was real or supplied by his licentious thoughts.

But she wasn't something new. Only his way of seeing her was new, and that wasn't what she was offering. Or was it? It wasn't the brulee that tempted him. "I'm not hungry."

"It's exquisite. You'll regret this decision later," Phoebe teased. "See if I offer you any more of my mango." She nibbled at the fruit, then licked the creamy custard off the spoon with delicate precision and a fantasy-inducing attention to detail.

His heart pounded like a jackhammer while an alarm sounded in his head. Kiki pushed a button on her watch, and the alarm stopped. Oh.

"Nine o'clock. I have to check in with the California office before they leave." Kiki stood.

Ryan pushed his chair back. "I'll go with you." It beat the hell out of staying for more erotic mango brulee torment.

Kiki waved for him to stay. "There's no need. I may be five minutes or it could be forty-five. You'll be bored."

"But—"

She pressed him back into his seat. "Stay and finish your wine. I'll meet you guys at the Jungle Room. Besides, I wouldn't mind a little privacy to freshen up."

She offered him very little choice but to stay. "Fine. The Jungle Room. I'll look for you."

"I may be a little late."

"Don't worry, Kiki. We'll take care of him until you get there," Phoebe teased with a hint of provocation.

She'd definitely noticed Kiki's monopoly of Elliott over dinner.

Kiki's eyes narrowed, and she dropped Phoebe a wink. "Thanks, Phoebe." She eyed Elliott. "I'll catch up with you all later. By then, I'll be ready to try out the limbo stick and see how low I can go."

Elliott watched Kiki's wiggling behind as she crossed the restaurant. He shook his head in admiration. "She's something else. Refill, anyone?" He reached for the bottle of wine with an alcohol-induced grin. "We'll have a full-fledged Caribbean bacchanalia."

Phoebe held her glass out, deepening her cleavage. "Just a touch, thanks."

Ryan accepted another half glass, as well. God knows, he didn't want Elliott to level off without a drinking buddy. The idea of Elliott passing out nightly suited Ryan just fine. If he was passed out, he wasn't up to bedroom games with Phoebe. Ryan assured himself the idea held such appeal simply because it put Phoebe one step further away from Elliott as a suitable husband.

"Can you believe Kiki knows Dean Whatley?" Ryan had no idea who Dean Whatley was and didn't much care. "They go way back." Elliott refueled with a full glass of wine.

"How does she know Dean Whatley?" Phoebe asked.

It was the only prompting Elliott needed to drone and drink. He polished off the bottle, his speech growing increasingly exact. He enunciated succinctly when he spilled the last of the red wine down the front of his white shirt. "Sod the dog."

Martin appeared immediately, a wet cloth in hand. "Most unfortunate. Let me help." He dabbed at the stain blooming on Elliott's shirtfront. "Might I recommend our most excellent laundry so that you do not ruin this shirt? Shall I send someone from housekeeping to collect this from you?"

"Fine." Elliott pushed to his feet, steadying himself against the table. "Great. Now I have to change my shirt. I'll meet you in the Jungle Room, too."

Elliott huffed off.

Martin nodded sagely. "Ah, the Jungle Room. A most excellent choice."

Ryan's body quickened as he recalled Phoebe's sensuous movements of the previous night.

Phoebe laughed, low and husky. The sound skittered down Ryan's spine. "Is everything always a most excellent choice, Martin?"

"Unfortunately not." Ryan could've sworn Martin glanced toward Elliott's retreating figure. "But I enjoy pointing out the ones that are, such as your hair." He bowed at the waist. "If you will excuse me."

Phoebe turned to Ryan and propped her elbow on the table, resting her chin on her hand. "Am I just being sensitive or have Kiki and Elliott formed a mutual admiration club?"

"You noticed too, huh?" Had she also noticed how close she'd come to killing Ryan over dessert?

"Yeah. I'd have to be dead to miss it." She smiled wryly.

"I suppose you're reconsidering Hot Sands as a potential honeymoon site?" Elliott was a goner. Ryan hoped like hell she'd given up her crazy marriage notion.

"Hot Sands is great. However, I'll be going back to the drawing board on groom material."

Relief filled him. It wasn't the whole wedding, but it was a start. She couldn't have a wedding without a groom. "Damn glad to hear you're dumping Elliott."

"I didn't say I was dumping him. I just know for sure I don't want to marry him."

She was dumping him.

Ryan felt better than he had in weeks. Everything would soon be back to normal. "Want to check out the beach before we meet them at the club?"

Phoebe smiled, the sexy gap between her two front teeth knotting his belly. Her eyes glittered smoky brown in the glow of the candle. "That sounds like a most excellent suggestion."

He stood and pulled out her chair. His hand brushed against the bare satin of her back as she stood. Fire licked through him at the brief touch.

Perhaps *everything* wouldn't be back to normal as soon as he thought.

"JUST LEAN ON ME." Ryan slid his arm around Phoebe's waist as she hobbled along the sidewalk, favoring her throbbing right ankle. She stumbled to a stop beside one of the flickering tiki torches that lent a primal feel to the night. His warm breath stirred against her neck, and his scent wrapped around her in the heat of the night. Laughter and throbbing music spilled out from the Jungle Room and blended with the nocturnal noises of insects and birds and whatever else rustled in the dark tropics, lending an intense intimacy to the right.

She wasn't so sure she'd be able to stop at leaning. She had the most insane, inopportune, politically incorrect, powerful urge to kiss him and see if the passion that had exploded between them last night had been real.

Wouldn't it make for a Kodak moment if Kiki or Elliott happened along while she put the moves on her best friend, who would most likely be horrified that she'd lost her mind and was flinging herself at him? It was one thing to test the waters with mild flirtation at a table for four or on a crowded dance floor, but there was no safety in numbers now.

"Phoebes? You're not about to faint, are you?"

"No. I'm not going to faint." Nor was she about to fall on him like some sex-starved harpy. And her ankle wasn't nearly as sore as her pride. "At least it was dark and nobody saw me fall off my shoe. Whatever possessed me to try and walk in the sand wearing platform sandals?" The offending shoe and its mate dangled from her right hand.

"Maybe because those shoes look hot with that short dress." His words played havoc with her pulse rate

and made her long for things she had no business longing for. "At least until you fell off of them."

"I only fell off one," Phoebe amended, a small salve
to her pride.

His teeth gleamed in the flickering torchlight. "I
stand corrected."

Competitiveness led her to ask, under the cover of
the sultry, inky night, "Do you think my legs are better
than—"

His grin faded. His face tightened in the torch glow.
"Anyone's. Your legs leave a man weak." No amusement lightened the rough cadence of his declaration.
"Now either lean on me or I'll pick you up and carry
you."

She didn't think so. There was nothing sexy about
indignity—his arm wrapped around the back of her
thighs, him staggering along the sidewalk beneath her
Amazonian proportions. Coupled with the disturbing
realization that she was beginning to crave his touch
like an addict needed a fix. "You wouldn't da—"

"Easy, Phoebes." His arm tightened around her
waist, and his voice dropped to a husky caress, sliding
along her nerve endings like verbal foreplay. She reminded herself of all the practice he'd had at hitting
just the right note. "You know I can't resist a dare."

She tried to relax into him. For as long as she could
remember, she and Ryan had propped one another up
in time of need. The press of his hip and thigh against
hers should've been reassuringly familiar. Instead it
aroused her, evoking a disquieting ripple of longing

that tightened inside her. He'd always been so attuned to her nuances. Could he feel her hunger for him? She pulled away. "I'm fine."

"If that's the way you want to play it." In one swift movement, he scooped her off her feet.

Time slowed to seconds of infinite awareness. Every inch of her responded to him. The brush of his hair-roughened arms against the sensitive backs of her knees and her back, bared by her halter top. The rise and fall of the hard wall of his chest against her right breast. His firm abs against her hip. The frantic beat of his heart against her arm.

His pupils dilated, darkened. Emotions, once so clearly defined between them, tangled, wrapped around them, between them, binding them with thick, sweet cords of promise.

"Put your arms around my neck," he instructed hoarsely.

In some distant recess of her mind, the idea niggled that she should demand he put her back on solid ground. However, the other part of her acknowledged how much she liked being swept off her feet in the beguiling shadows of a Jamaican night and held tight against him. She looped her arms around the strong column of his neck and tucked her head into the crook of his shoulder without a word.

She expected him to stagger forward beneath her weight, shattering their dreamlike intimacy. Instead, he strode forward effortlessly. "Your room or mine?"

The night. His suggestive words. His scent. The

rough edge to his question. Phoebe reminded herself this was Ryan and he only intended to examine her ankle.

His room was just ahead. Hers was on the west wing. The sooner he put her down, the better. "Yours. It's closer than mine. And there's a good chance Elliott's passed out." She didn't want to think about Elliott while Ryan's solid strength melted her from the inside out.

He stopped outside his room and fished out his room card, still holding her. A muted giggle sounded on the other side of the door. "Kiki must still be on the phone," Ryan murmured, his mouth mere inches from her ear.

Ryan toed open the door and angled inside.

Unaware of an audience, flat on her back in a tangle of sheets and limbs, Kiki squealed. The door clicked shut behind them.

What the.... Phoebe looked at Ryan. "She's not on the phone."

Kiki's head popped up. Her subsequent squeal echoed the surprise on her face at seeing Ryan and Phoebe. Midway on the bed, Elliott's dark head poked out from beneath the sheet.

All the air swooshed out of her. She had recognized the obvious attraction between Kiki and Elliott, but she hadn't expected *this*.

Phoebe slid down the front of Ryan to stand, one arm still wrapped around his neck. Not only was Elliott in bed, naked, she presumed, with another woman, but given his position, she didn't need Kiki's quantum physics degree to figure out what he'd been doing. Only he'd never been willing to do *that* for *her*.

Ryan raised a sardonic brow. "And he's not passed out."

"SORRY, GUYS. We just sort of hit it off." Kiki delivered the understatement of the year. "Hope you're not too wigged out."

"Come on in." Elliott lifted the edge of the sheet in leering invitation. "Two's a couple, three's a crowd, but four's a party."

And this was the man she'd barely managed to budge out of the missionary position? Phoebe had counted on Jamaica loosening Elliott up. But she wasn't ready for this loose. Ryan wrapped a thick arm about her waist in support. "Thanks, but no thanks." Ryan declined on their behalf.

Phoebe laughed, hoping no one noticed the faint echo of hysteria in her voice. "I'm not much of a party girl."

Kiki shot her an arch look. "Now, Phoebe, I know you're wrong about that. I saw you on the dance floor. Don't be coy. And although you and Ryan denied anything last night, I've seen the way you look at one another when no one else is looking. Why else would two couples head down here together if they weren't interested in a swap and swing meet?"

That had never occurred to her. She wasn't particularly old-fashioned and she didn't have sexual hang-ups, she simply wasn't a group-sex kind of girl.

"It'll put a little spark back in our relationship, Phoebe," Elliott wheedled.

"It could be a lot of fun," Kiki coaxed. "The four of us. And you did tell me at dinner tonight you'd take care of Ryan."

Just because she'd thought Kiki deserved a little verbal payback for so obviously playing up to Elliott. It hadn't meant she would hop into bed with her best friend. Her hand itched to slap that seductive look off of Kiki's face.

"Fun's a relative issue." Ryan shook his head, his eyes hard despite the studied amusement on his face. "I don't like to share with others."

Elliott blanched.

Although Phoebe felt a bit naive and gauche in view of Kiki's sexual sophistication, this was one game she had no interest in playing. Or at least not by Kiki and Elliott's rules. She wasn't about to be dumped on. She'd set her own rules. A slow smile spread over her face. She turned to Ryan, throwing them into full body contact.

Surprise flared in his eyes. Insinuating her leg between his thighs, she leaned against him and silently willed him to go out for a long pass. A thread of tension wound through her that had nothing to do with their audience. "We obviously don't have to worry about how or when to break the news to them, darling."

Ryan caught the ball and ran with it. He brought his other arm around her, sliding his hand over her hip to settle on her behind. "Most excellent timing, in fact."

For a moment, Phoebe lost herself in the simmering heat of his eyes, the muscular length of his body pressed against her and his marauding hand on her bottom. She was a woman being held by a very sexy man.

"What news?" Elliott scowled from the bed, compounding his lack of good judgment—choosing Kiki over Phoebe—with offense.

"Kiki's right about one thing. Phoebe and I realized earlier today there's something much more intense than friendship between us. Something hot and explosive." Even though Ryan directed his words to Kiki and Elliott, his eyes never left Phoebe's face.

She licked at her suddenly dry lips. It was closer to the truth than he knew. "We weren't sure how or when to tell you." She managed to utter the words.

"I've barely been able to keep my hands off her all evening." Ryan smoothed his palm up her buttocks and along her back until he touched the skin bared by her halter dress. "Now I don't have to."

His touch trailed fire along her sensitized nerve endings. His pale green eyes mesmerized her. For a second, they were all alone in the room.

"Phoebe! How could you do something like this to me? I'm shocked," Elliott protested.

She was pretty shocked herself.

"I'm not." Kiki pouted. "I told you I saw the way they looked at one another earlier."

Damn if these two didn't have some nerve to embrace outrage—while they rolled around naked under the covers together. Apparently the two of them falling into bed together or the four of them cavorting under the covers was acceptable, but Phoebe and Ryan getting together on their own was an insult. Phoebe was doubly glad she and Ryan had turned the tables on them.

"You look as if you're dealing with your shock," Ryan noted with more than a touch of sarcasm. "I think you'll both recover quickly."

Phoebe pasted on a contrite expression. "I'm really sorry, Elliott. This thing between us..." She brushed her mouth against Ryan's, her eyes locked in the green depth of his. Despite her performance for an audience, a shiver crawled over her skin. "It's overwhelming." She glanced at Elliott. "Look at it this way. You're not left high and dry. At least you two get the consolation prize."

Kiki's mouth tightened. "Now, wait a minute, sister—"

Phoebe cut her off at the pass. "I understand you're upset. I'd be upset in your position, as well." Phoebe eyed Kiki in the bed with Elliott. "But there are so few good men out there, you just have to take one when you finally find him." She rubbed her head against Ryan's chin. "Even if he's been there all along."

His smoldering look left her trembling. "I'm ready

for some privacy, now that we've got this out of the way." Ryan opened the door and looked at Elliott. "I'll be back in just a minute with your clothes and then I'll get my suitcase."

Elliott pushed the sheet aside, as if to pack for himself. "I don't want my shirts wrinkled."

"Please." Ryan threw up a hand. "Do us all a favor. Don't get up."

5

"I CHECKED at the front desk and even tracked down Martin to see if he could help us out." Ryan tossed his suitcase on the upholstered chaise. "It's a no go on an extra room. They've got a few empty rooms, but they're under renovation. Everything else is booked. Looks like we're roommates for the rest of the week."

Elliott had surpassed Ryan's expectations. Ryan had thought Elliott would hold steady with some heavy flirting. He'd been damned surprised to find Kiki and Elliott bumping uglies.

Ryan tugged his shirttail free. Things had gone much further than he anticipated. He damn sure hadn't bargained to share a room with Phoebe. Phoebe, who was slowly driving him crazy.

She nibbled at her lower lip and shrugged, failing dismally at appearing nonchalant. "Not a big deal. How many nights have you crashed at my house before?"

That was before he'd touched her as a man instead of a friend. Before he knew the hot, sweet taste of her mouth. Before this throbbing awareness of each other as a man and a woman pulsed between them. And crashing at her place was a far cry from this opulent room with its king-size bed that begged for sex.

"Sure. Not a big deal." He called on all his resolve. "We can handle it."

"Absolutely." She didn't look any surer than he felt. "And it certainly makes our story of newly discovered passion more valid if we're actually in the same room."

Ryan grinned at her wry assessment, "I guess it's a good thing you're quick-witted with a competitive streak a mile wide." He unbuttoned his cuffs. "You need to get off that ankle."

Phoebe ignored him and paced to the French doors and back, her dress hugging her delectable rear. "Can you believe they were in bed together? In my book, it's far better to be the dumper than the dumpee. Even though things were on the down slide with Elliott, there's no way Kiki's going to walk away thinking she stole him." Phoebe planted her hands on her hips, her competitive ire up. "Even if she did. And of course, you didn't fare any better at Elliott's hands."

Ryan read her hurt beneath the bravado. Striking Elliott off the marriage list was one thing. Finding him in bed with another woman was another. In the warm glow of the bedside lamp, she was a stirring mixture of indignity and vulnerability. Just looking at her standing beside the bed filled him with a longing so fierce it left him breathless.

As a rule, he never felt fierce about anything. "That's strictly a matter of opinion. I definitely wound up with the best. Elliott's a fool."

"Spoken like a true best friend."

Was that an affirmation or a reminder? He'd never lied to Phoebe and he wasn't going to start now. And a smidgen of guilt for encouraging Kiki and Elliott prodded him to come clean.

"Spoken like a man." His quiet words hung between them.

Irreversible.

Provocative.

Her eyes held his with an intensity that left him breathless. "Kiki's the fool."

"They have a lot in common." The comfort he ached to give her wasn't what she needed. Ryan stepped toward her. "Get on the bed, Phoebe."

Color stained her cheeks. "Ryan, we can't... I don't think..."

Was that a combination of guilt, confusion and lust clouding her eyes? Or were those his emotions he saw reflected? "You need to get off your ankle."

"Oh. Right." She sank onto the mattress and swung her legs up, shifting over to make room for him. "How's that?"

"Fine." He was living proof that men were visually stimulated because he was so damn stimulated at her stretched out on the bed he could hardly stand himself. Exotic braids, satin smooth skin, legs that went on forever, coral-tipped toenails. She was one dress away from yesterday's beach fantasy.

"Do you want to look at it?" She turned her leg and winced.

Her question twisted him in knots. Her ankle. She meant her ankle. How would he ever last six nights in this room with her?

"Sure. Let's see what's going on." He turned his back to her and leaned on the edge of the bed facing her feet. A man could only stand so much torture. And with the short, tight fit of her dress... Her ankle was the only thing he was supposed to check out.

"Ryan?"

He glanced over his shoulder. "Yeah?"

"When they asked us to join them, were you tempted?"

He turned, carefully probing the tender skin of her ankle with his fingers. What tempted him would send her through the roof. "Were you?"

"I asked you first."

"No, I wasn't remotely interested. You?"

"The truth? I think I'm far too competitive for group sex. I'd be so busy trying to outperform, I couldn't really enjoy myself."

The delicate bones and smooth skin of her ankle were warm beneath his fingertips. He closed his eyes with a silent groan. Images flashed through his head, leaving him speechless and hard. He twisted on the bed and studied Phoebe, the high cheekbones, the dusting of freckles across the bridge of her nose, the faint ridge of a scar beneath her chin, earned when they built their backyard clubhouse at the ripe age of ten. He'd never cared for anyone the way he cared for

Phoebe. And he, of all people, knew caring and sex were two separate issues.

"What?" Her voice was breathy. Unsure.

He reached out and smoothed the pad of his thumb across her cheek. "All this time I've known you, I never noticed you have remarkable bone structure." Color washed the high ridge and warmed the skin beneath his finger.

"That's what Martin said." Uncertainty flickered across her face. "I thought he was just angling for a kickback."

"No. Martin was on to something." Was this exotic look a new image for her? "Are you going to keep the braids? When we go home?"

"No. It's an exciting change for a few days, but it would never fit in. I'll go back to the way it was before."

He wasn't Mr. Sensitivity, but he had the distinct impression they were talking about more than just her hair. "Some things may never go back to the way they were." Would he ever again meet Phoebe for lunch at Birelli's and not feel this powerful tug of attraction, like the dangerous undertow of a treacherous tide? And what was wrong with him? He never made cryptic observations.

She squared her shoulders and tilted her chin as if preparing for battle. "Would you have been interested if I hadn't been part of the equation?"

Couldn't she feel the yearning for her that gnawed at him? "You're kidding, right?"

"Do you see me laughing, Ryan?"

No. Vulnerability and intensity shadowed her sherry-brown eyes.

"I don't like to share."

"Oh."

"I prefer making love one-on-one." His eyes held hers. "Undivided attention. No distractions." He could barely think beyond wanting to do just that with her. "But that's just me. And for the record, you were the only part of that equation that held any interest for me."

His raw admission hung between them. Bare. Open.

Phoebe dragged in a deep, shuddering breath. "So, what do you recommend for my ankle, Dr. Palmer?"

He hadn't expected her to launch herself at him, and she hadn't. But with the pretense gone, perhaps they could make it through the week. He read her we-can't-go-there message loud and clear.

"Let's elevate and ice it." Ryan grabbed a pillow. "You should be okay by tomorrow." Phoebe shifted her ankle to her pillow, inadvertently offering Ryan a view of sun-kissed thighs beneath the hem of her short white dress.

He straightened abruptly. A man could only take so much. "I'll go get ice for an ice pack. Why don't you change into your pajamas while I'm gone?" Otherwise he was in serious danger of forgetting those gorgeous thighs were attached to Phoebe. Baggy boxers and a worn T-shirt, Phoebe's standard sleepwear, would, he hoped, give his blood pressure more of a break than her sexy, short dress.

"But it's still early."

"Yeah. And if you take care of this tonight, you should be all better by tomorrow. If you don't, you could wind up blowing the whole week."

"Okay. You're right." She huffed out a breath, and his heart threatened to stop as her breasts heaved against her plunging neckline. "Go ahead and go out without me. I'll be fine here."

No way he'd leave her in the room alone to work herself into a state over Elliott. And it wouldn't be any fun without her, anyway. "Forget it. We're in this together. Anyway, what if I ran into Kiki and Elliott? How can I be out hitting the bars when I'm supposedly in bed with you?"

"Oh, yeah. Right."

He headed for the door. "Ice. Coming right up."

Unfortunately, so were other things.

PHOEBE LIMPED out of the bathroom, determined to regain some measure of equanimity before Ryan returned.

I prefer making love one-on-one...no distractions...you were the only part of the equation that held any interest for me.

Friends. Friends. Friends. She repeated the word over and over to banish the echo of his tempting phrases, the memory of his fingers against her skin and the heat in his green eyes. Awareness rumbled between them like some great beast begging to be unleashed.

He opened the door.

"Ice." He hoisted the ice bucket and crossed the room without looking at her. "Why don't you prop your ankle up on the pillows again while I make an icepack?"

A nervous shiver passed over her skin as she settled on the bed. While he fashioned an ice pack out of a plastic laundry bag he found in the closet, she studied the familiar set of his broad shoulders. Even though he looked the same as her Ryan, this was a different man. Or, more aptly, a different facet of the man she knew. Secondhand exposure to his carnality was vastly different than coming face-to-face with his desire.

She tugged the scoop neck of her tank top up further. Ryan had seen her ready for bed any number of times. But she hadn't packed sweats, boxers or oversize T-shirts on this trip. She'd armed herself with a suitcase of seduction. At Victoria's Secret, they now knew her by name and American Express account number.

Bronze satin tap pants and a matching scooped tank top were the most sedate things she'd brought along. She gave the top another tug. Maybe Ryan wouldn't notice it barely covered her.

He turned, wrapping a hand towel around the ice-filled bag. He glanced up and stopped mid-stride. His face flushed, and he sucked in a ragged breath.

Her pulse hammered so hard it left her breathless.

He'd noticed.

"Where are your boxers? Your T-shirt?" The low gravel of his voice pebbled her nipples to hard points. "I'll get them for you."

"I didn't bring any." Phoebe wavered between gratification and dismay. Finding Elliott in bed with Kiki had delivered a none-too-subtle message that her ex-boyfriend had found her lacking. Her ego was wide open to a healthy dose of male appreciation. But this was Ryan.

"You're probably cold." Actually, she was very, very hot after seeing the look in his eyes. "Why don't I grab your robe for you? Just tell me where it is and I'll get it." His harsh desperation fanned the flame inside her, heightened her sensitivity to the play of satin against her buttocks and between her thighs, the cling of her stretchy top to her breasts and their aching crests.

"I didn't bring a robe." Her husky tone seemed to threaten his control.

He closed his eyes and clenched his jaw. "I'm going to open my eyes in five seconds. If you know what's best for both of us, you'll be under the covers then."

She was there in three, leaving her ankle out and propped on the pillow, trying to relax between the soft brush of cotton sheets.

Ryan opened his eyes, his expression bland, the fire in his eyes gone. If she didn't know better, she would think she'd imagined the whole thing.

"This should help." He settled the ice pack on her tender ankle and adjusted the pillow beneath her lower leg. His square, capable hands trembled against her skin, giving lie to his composure and destroying hers. The scent of Ryan's cologne wrapped around her. Need coiled between them. Heat rolled through her. She wanted him with an intensity that left her shaking.

She moved her leg away from his touch. "That's fine. Thank you."

He stepped away from the bed, and Phoebe struggled to regain her control.

She laughed, the sound strained even to her ears. "This isn't quite what I planned. Propped up in bed with a bum ankle..."

"Finding your boyfriend with my girlfriend?" Ryan turned his back to her and began to unbutton his shirt.

Wanting him to the point of distraction...

"No, that was definitely not part of the plan." She watched him in the dresser mirror. Golden-brown hair sprinkled his chest and narrowed to disappear beneath his pants.

He looked up and caught her watching him. Wanting him. Without a word he strode to the bathroom and closed the door.

Phoebe turned out the light and willed sanity to return.

Ryan was her friend. She needed to remember that.

Ryan had a terrible track record with women. She definitely needed to remember that.

Ryan's touch set her on fire. That would get her in deep trouble.

MMM. Phoebe shifted, snuggling closer to the solid warmth beneath her cheek and against her thigh as she drifted out of the depths of a deep, dreamless sleep. A familiar and arousing scent seeped into her consciousness. Layers of sleep fell away. She woke to the of the weight of a male leg thrown over her. The tickle of chest hair against her breast. The hardened length of a man...

Her eyes flew open. Her. Ryan. Entwined. They'd started out on opposite sides of the king-size bed last night. During the night they'd definitely found each other in the middle. Steady, even breathing—thank God he was still asleep.

The sensible thing to do would be to extricate herself immediately. And she would—in just a minute. What harm could possibly come from a few minutes of sensual indulgence?

She closed her eyes and absorbed the feel of him. The muscular length of his pajama-clad legs tangled with hers. The tease of his springy chest hair against her bared nipple. The ripple of his belly beneath her hand. Ryan's thickly muscled arm pillowed her head. The hard ridge of his erection, confined by his pajama bottoms, pressed against her thigh. His warm breath stirred against the back of her scalp.

Languid, liquid desire flowed through her, filled her. Nestled in his arms, Phoebe realized she'd never truly known desire before now. What she'd thought desire had been mere sexual arousal.

Ryan was her desire.

Ryan was also her best friend.

She flexed her fingers against his flat stomach, exulting in the texture of his skin, his male scent. The feather-light brush of his chest hair against the tight bud of her breast left her wet and aching.

He wanted her as desperately as she wanted him. She'd seen the heat in his eyes, heard the hoarse want in his voice. The easy thing to do would be to wake him by slipping her hand beneath the drawstring waist of his pajamas and wrapping her fingers around him while she flicked her tongue against his flat male nipple.

Phoebe closed her eyes. The realm of friendship offered safety. She was there for him, and he was there for her. But there was nothing safe about Ryan as a lover. How many times had she seen him go from one woman to another? He'd never intentionally hurt her, but he could devastate her nonetheless.

She'd never planned for this to happen. She didn't have a plan for how to deal with this. But there was a world of difference between the easy thing to do and the right thing to do.

She untangled her leg from between his and tugged her top into place. Moving carefully, she rolled to her other side and inched toward the edge of the mattress. Ryan made disgruntled sleeping noises and rolled over behind her, curling his arm around her neck and across her chest. His other arm wrapped around her from behind, effectively trapping her. Like a homing device, his erection found her backside.

She should move. Jump. Run. Take action. Instead, she instinctively wriggled against him. His right hand slid to her breast, cupping it in his big palm. With lazy, somnolent movements, he rolled her nipple between his fingers. Exquisite sensation arrowed through her. Behind her, his warm mouth nuzzled against the sensitive juncture of her neck and shoulder. A low moan escaped her.

She knew the second Ryan gained some semblance of consciousness. His hand toying with her nipple stilled, and his entire body grew rigid. "Phoebe? Phoebe, are you awake?"

How could she roll over and say yes? Phoebe stretched out of his arms, pretending to wake up. "Hmm? What?"

She avoided looking at Ryan as she catapulted off the side of the bed. "I've got the shower first."

She slammed the door behind her and leaned against it, filled with equal measures of longing and self-loathing.

RYAN FINISHED UP quickly in the bathroom. He'd showered the night before. A long, cold stinging shower before he crawled into bed with Phoebe, his best friend and tormentor. He pulled on his swim trunks and walked into the room.

"Ready for some breakfast?" Phoebe's voice rang overbright and brittle. She hadn't looked at him since she'd showered and dressed.

He ought to feel really, really bad. He'd groped his

best friend this morning while she lay sleeping. Unfortunately, he'd enjoyed the hell out of it. He could still taste the sweet warmth of her shoulder against his lips, feel the lean line of her back against the wall of his chest, the tease of her buttocks against his hard-on.

"Breakfast sounds good. How's your ankle?"

Phoebe brushed past him. The brief contact and her freshly showered fragrance left him aching.

She slipped into a pair of sandals and wiggled her foot. "Much better. Just an occasional twinge."

"Are you up for snorkeling this morning? The boat leaves the pier in an hour and a half. I put us on the list while you were showering."

"Absolutely." Phoebe squared her shoulders. "Now remember, when we see Kiki and Elliott, we need to lay it on thick."

He could still feel the swell of her breast with its crested tip in the palm of his hand. He wasn't sure how much thicker he could handle. "Are you sure you don't want to just let it go?"

"They dumped us and hopped in bed together practically in front of us. How can you even consider letting it go?"

There was no swaying Phoebe when she went into her hypercompetitive mode. "Right. We'll lay it on thick."

Six more days and five long, hot nights. He just needed to remember Phoebe wasn't like other women, she was...well, Phoebe. Although exactly why Phoebe being Phoebe was a problem was beginning to blur for him, lost in the haze of haunting want.

He slung an arm around her shoulders when they left the room, her breast a tantalizing reach away from his fingertips. The sway of her hip against his, the press of her arm about his waist, the brush of her braids against his shoulder, proved sweet torture as they walked to the waterside restaurant.

The translucent blue-green waters of the Caribbean sparkled beneath the clear azure sky. Early morning sunbathers lined up their chaises along the white sand, avoiding the shade cast by the tall palms. A couple, their arms wound about one another, walked along the edge of the surf. Despite the people, spindle-legged sandpipers darted on the wet sand. From the carefully tended garden, the mournful call of doves echoed among the raucous cry of parrots.

"It's another beautiful day in paradise, isn't it?" Phoebe offered quietly, uncannily giving voice to his thoughts as they entered the open-air restaurant they both favored.

Breakfast was an informal affair where they seated themselves. A buffet offering a smorgasbord of breakfast items lined the back rail.

Ryan spotted Kiki and Elliott the moment they entered the restaurant. "Don't look now, but the enemy's at two o'clock."

Phoebe didn't bother to scan the room. She immediately attached herself to him like a limpet.

The same river of desire he'd almost drowned in earlier flooded through him again.

She nuzzled his jaw, her lips mere millimeters from his ear. "Come on, Ryan. You need to look at me as if we just rolled out of bed and you can't wait to get me back there again."

"Maybe that's closer to the truth than you know," he murmured against her mouth, tasting the hint of mint toothpaste clinging to her lips. He slipped his arm around her waist and splayed his fingers against her hip.

They crossed the room, lucking into a table next to the water. Ryan sat next to Phoebe, instead of across the table, as if he couldn't bear to be that far away from her, which was the case. He caught her hand in his, gratified by her swift intake of breath.

Martin appeared with his ready smile. "I regret that I could not be of more service last night. How is everything this morning?" He looked at their clasped hands and beamed. "Ah, it appears you weathered the evening."

"Yes. It's a beautiful morning on your island." Ryan had given Martin the right to inquire by seeking his help last night.

"We actually see it quite a bit. Two couples who come together and leave with the other." He smiled mysteriously. "It is the magic of the island. It casts a spell and brings out the truth of the heart." Martin laughed. "Ah, I see by your face's expression you do not believe in the magic of Jamaica. Once I did not believe, as well. Until the magic brought me my most excellent wife."

Phoebe leaned forward, interest lighting her expressive face. She was breathtakingly beautiful. "I would love to hear how you met Mathilde. Wouldn't you, Ryan?"

"Absolutely." Ryan personally thought Martin, although a nice guy, was fully capable of spinning a tale or two for the tourists' entertainment.

"Mathilde and I used to play stickball together. We grew up in the same village. We were friends, but I did not truly see Mathilde's excellence until I spent the season of my nineteenth year working in Negril to prepare for my position here. When I returned, a new man in our village was courting Mathilde. It was then, through the island's magic, that I truly saw her and we came to be married."

Ryan shifted in his chair. Martin's story struck uncomfortably close to home. And look where it had gotten Martin—married. Tied to one woman. It sounded as if Martin had taken action to protect his interest. But if Martin wanted to call it island magic, who was Ryan to disagree?

A hint of panic flared in Phoebe's eyes. Did she recognize the similarities, as well? "That's a lovely story, Martin. What were you like growing up? Quiet? Shy?"

Martin preened a bit and shrugged. "I was quite the lady's man in my younger days. My Mathilde had become disgusted with me. But that is enough about me. May I bring you some of Jamaica's most excellent Blue

Mountain coffee? It is on the buffet, but I will bring a
fresh pot for you."

"Thank you."

"It is my pleasure. And might I suggest the akee and
pain au chocolat when you visit the buffet. Both are ex-
ceptional today."

Martin went for their coffee. Ryan pushed his chair
back and stood. "Wait here and I'll make a plate." He
stilled her protest with a finger against her lips. "Rest
your ankle. Don't worry. I know what you like."

She settled into her chair. "Okay. Only a crazy
woman would turn down being waited on. Thank
you."

Ryan quickly returned. He'd filled one plate with
chunks of mango and papaya, akee, naseberries, ba-
nanas and a pear-shaped Otaheite apple. The other
plate held an assortment of pastries.

While he was gone, Martin had brought and served
their coffee. The aroma of roasted coffee mingled with
the heavy sweetness of ripe fruit and light, yeasty
pastries.

Phoebe longingly eyed the pastry plate. "Ryan, you
know I can't resist that, but I don't need it."

"It's your vacation, Phoebes. Indulge. Go back to
your diet when we return to Nashville." He tore the
pain au chocolat in half. Dark chocolate oozed from the
croissant's buttery layers onto his fingers.

She reached for a chunk of papaya. Before she could
bring the fruit to her mouth, he leaned close—until he
saw blue sky reflected in her black irises. Ryan offered

the morsel before her pink parted lips. Slowly, deliberately, she sank her white teeth into the flaky pastry and rich chocolate. The clink of silverware and the hum of conversation dimmed, lost in the rushing of his blood as she stroked her moist tongue along the length of his finger, licking the chocolate off him. With that one stroke of her tongue, he thickened and lengthened.

"Chocolate and fruit. One of my favorites." The husky cadence of her voice tempted him, as rich and inviting as the chocolate. Her eyes held his as she brought the papaya to her mouth. She closed her lips around part of the pink-hued flesh, its sweet, sticky juice coating her lips.

The hardened points of her nipples poked at the soft cotton of her cover-up. She was as turned on as he was. Ryan groaned, unsure he'd actually live through breakfast with her.

She held the other half of the fruit to his lips, her bite marks scoring the fruit. "Try it," she invited, sliding the ripe tidbit into his mouth. Firm, yet succulent. He savored the juicy sweetness against his tongue. His body throbbed in response.

He'd never dreamed that eating breakfast with Phoebe would turn into a barely decent experience.

6

PHOEBE STOOD on the side of the boat and checked her mask and snorkel, the sun warm on her shoulders and back. All around them, the sea shimmered like thick-fired glass hued with greens and blues. Below the surface, corals and fronds of sea grass swayed in the current. Reggae played over the boat's speakers.

Beside her, Ryan pulled off his shirt. Phoebe was more than ready to snorkel. Not only was she eager to explore the tropical waters, she was desperate for a measure of relief from this tension binding her to Ryan. They'd always been close, but this was a deeper, primal connection. She still wasn't sure what had happened at breakfast. What had begun as a show for Kiki and Elliott had wound up a seduction of the senses. Even now, every nerve in her body responded to his nearness, the rhythm of his breathing, his scent, the heat of his body. Surely, the water would afford some relief from this aching awareness.

The music stopped abruptly and a high-pitched squeal rent the air as the boat captain, a small wiry man with a sun-weathered face, picked up a microphone.

"Welcome to some of the finest snorkeling in Jamaica. Before you get in the water, it is necessary for us to go over a few things. Remember, do not touch the coral. It is a living thing and you do not want to damage the reef. This is important." He paused to make sure everyone heard.

"Please snorkel with a partner. This is for your safety. Also, in the interest of safety, take care not to swim past the orange markers. The reef does not extend past that point, but boats do. Being run over by a boat is a bad way to end your holiday." A titter ran through the small group on the boat.

"We have snacks and refreshments on board for you. Feel free to help yourself. Finally, there is a rumor that Blackbeard sank a Spanish galleon in these waters." He threw his hands in the air, palms up, shrugging. "Should you find any wreckage, please let us know. We will be here for two hours. Enjoy the beautiful treasures of the Caribbean Sea."

"Are you ready? Your treasures await, sea princess." Ryan's ready, easy smile accompanied his banter.

"Just let me put on my clown feet." Phoebe perched on the side of the boat and tugged on her flippers.

He shook his head, the sun glinting off strands of hair already bleached by the bright rays. The banked fire in his gaze slid over her, heating her.

"No, Phoebes. You're definitely a sea princess. An exotic mermaid with a siren's call, luring sailors into your mysterious depths with the promise of exploring your treasures."

Phoebe could barely breathe. The low strum of his voice. The erotic imagery provoked by his words. It was verbal lovemaking on the open sea with the sun on her back and the caress of the wind against her skin.

"Lead on, princess. I'll willingly follow you," Ryan continued.

Not only was she fairly sure she was incapable of speech, but what could she possibly say to that? Silently, she slid into the waiting arms of the water, sinking completely below the surface into the wet embrace. Ryan slipped into the water beside her.

She surfaced and donned her mask and snorkel. "Are you sure you're willing to follow me, sailor?"

"Always."

Phoebe inserted her mouthpiece, took him by the hand and led him to another world below the surface. Viewed from above, it was intriguing, but below the surface the reef revealed its true intensity and vibrancy—a surreal landscape of unsurpassed beauty. Together they explored canyons and caves of bright, vivid corals in a variety of shapes and sizes, swam through schools of vibrant tropical fish.

Ryan directed her attention to the sandy ocean floor. A manta ray stirred, betraying its camouflaged position. Exhibiting grace and speed, it fled its ocean bed and glided past them.

Even when they were surrounded by the water, awareness pulsed between them, enfolding them in their own private world. The hours passed like minutes. Phoebe was astonished when Ryan tapped his waterproof watch, signaling their time was up.

Together they rose to the surface. Phoebe slid her mask off. "That was absolutely fantastic."

Ryan grinned, pulling her to the boat's ladder with him. "It was, wasn't it?"

They climbed aboard, returned their gear and settled on a cushioned seat next to one another. What a special experience, in large part due to Ryan's presence. She wouldn't have enjoyed snorkeling nearly as much with Elliott.

"Thank you." She plucked two towels off the stack supplied by the resort and passed one to Ryan.

He rubbed the thick towel over his chest, dislodging droplets of water caught in the golden-brown hair. "Thanks for what?"

Phoebe stared as a rivulet of water trailed along his tanned, muscled bicep. She longed to lick the wet brine off his fine-textured, sun-heated skin and savor the taste of him against her tongue. Instead, she blotted her dripping braids with her towel, disconcerted by the depth of yearning Ryan invoked in her. She'd never felt this compulsion with Elliott or any boyfriend before him. She might be losing her mind, but she refused to lose her best friend to this. Through sheer will, she marshaled her thoughts. What had she thanked him for?

"For signing us up for the snorkeling. I've never seen anything so beautiful."

He dragged the towel over the flat planes of his belly with mesmerizing deliberation. His eyes darkened and his gaze lingered on her face like a lover's touch. He leaned forward, his mouth only inches from her own. She recalled, with throbbing clarity, the heat of his mouth on hers that night inside the Jungle Room, his taste, the touch of his hands on her skin.

"I assure you, I've never seen anything more beautiful, either."

"PHOEBE. RYAN. Over here."

Phoebe glanced over her shoulder. Kiki waved from a poolside deck chair, motioning them over, Elliott by her side. Great.

Phoebe's nerves were already stretched to breaking point. She and Ryan had spent the afternoon on the beach after they returned from snorkeling. It should've been relaxing, soothing, calming. But the easy camaraderie she'd always shared with Ryan had been replaced by seething sexual awareness. Showering and changing for an early dinner had been worse, sharing the confines of a room designed to invite pleasure, both of them ignoring the want that throbbed between them.

"I suppose it's too late to pretend we didn't see them, huh?" Phoebe asked.

Ryan turned in Elliott and Kiki's direction. "So, do you think they'll ask us to join in a rousing round of naked twister?"

"With the two of them, it's a distinct possibility." Phoebe looked at Elliott. No ache filled her heart. Not even a slight tremor. No weak knees or feverish desire. Blast. She would've felt better if she'd had even one of those responses to his dark-eyed visage. No. Like some whacked-out cosmic joke, Ryan struck those chords for her.

Her body went on red alert when Ryan settled his hand against the small of her back, his fingers hot through the material of her dress.

"Hi, guys. We just wanted to make sure there were no hard feelings about last night," Kiki said.

Phoebe wrapped her arm around Ryan's waist. "Are you kidding? We were thinking about sending a bottle of champagne in thanks."

Elliott appeared suitably affronted. "You needn't be so bloody insulting about it."

"Sorry. We're both sort of giddy with having finally found one another. All this time..." Phoebe sighed into Ryan, and he nuzzled her forehead.

"Were you at the beach this morning?" Kiki asked.

"No, this afternoon. We spent the morning snorkeling. It was incredible. You guys should try it tomorrow."

Elliott shook his head. "Not tomorrow. We're heading over to the private island for some nude sunbathing. But then I don't imagine that would interest you. It's a bit uninhibited."

Did Elliott deliberately use that goading tone?

"Really? We might see you there. We're supposed to go, as well," Phoebe said.

"Unless we're otherwise distracted," Ryan amended with a tight smile. "I'm sure we'll see you around."

Ryan hustled Phoebe off in record time, practically

hauling her along. Instead of the restaurant, he headed toward their room.

"The restaurant's the other way."

"I know." Anger rolled off him in waves.

In silence, Ryan opened the room door. He wasn't, however, silent for long.

"We're not going to the topless beach tomorrow. *We* are not going at all. If you want to go, you'll have to go by yourself." Ryan exploded once their room door had closed behind them.

His vehemence surprised her. Easygoing, laid-back Ryan didn't lose his temper. "What's wrong with you? Why are you making such a big deal about nude sunbathing? Have you developed some sense of modesty? They're a bunch of strangers."

"For once, can't you just let it go, Phoebe?"

Phoebe seldom—well, more like never—heard that note of leashed frustration in Ryan's voice. "No. I can't just let it go." She narrowed her eyes as a totally loathsome idea came to mind. "Is it the idea of seeing Kiki and not being able to have her?"

Ryan advanced across the tile floor, every vestige of boyish good humor replaced by hard implacability. Her heart thudded against her breastbone, part trepidation, part excitement. "Let it go, Phoebe."

"I can't."

He stepped closer, his hands clenched at his sides. She refused to retreat, even though she felt caught in a storm brewing in the cauldron of emotion seething between them.

Ryan stood before her. Phoebe was painfully aware of him. The memory of awakening sprawled across him haunted her with painful clarity. "Talk to me," she said.

"Talk to you? You want me to talk to you?" The sliver of space between them pulsed with tension. "Goddamn it, Phoebe. That's the problem. I can't talk to you. I want you so bad I can hardly stand myself. I'll be damned if I'm going to look at you naked on some island tomorrow to prove some idiotic point. I'm not up for more looking but no touching unless Elliott and Kiki are around. And you want me to talk to you? This is about the only talk I'm up for right now."

He jerked her to him and cradled her head in his hands. Inexorably, he drew her mouth to his. A part of her hungered for the taste and feel of him. Another part of her screamed in protest. There was no audience. This was a kiss between a man and woman, a kiss of want and need. With unswerving surety, she knew this kiss would forever change their relationship. But Phoebe had spent the last few days running. And she didn't want to run anymore.

Her breath became his as he slanted his mouth over hers. She plied her lips against his in return, adrift in the taste of him, the feel of him. Drowning desire tugged at her with treacherous, dangerous undercurrents. Slowly she surfaced, gasping for air, her breath ragged.

"Maybe going to the topless beach isn't such a good idea, after all." Phoebe broke the heavy silence.

"This is the part where I'm supposed to say I'm sorry." Ryan dropped his hands to his sides. "But I'm not. I've wanted to do that all day."

"This is my fault. I started this last night when we found them—"

Ryan shook his head. "No. Maybe Martin was right. There is something magical about this place."

This was uncomfortable, but at least they were getting things out in the open. Phoebe, unfortunately, had a few truths to lay out on the table herself. She screwed up her courage. Confession was reportedly good for the soul. "I need to tell you something."

"Do I need to sit down?" Ryan asked with a wry grin.

"Only if you're tired." Phoebe paced to the other side of the room. "This morning, when you woke up, I wasn't asleep."

There it was, out in the open. Her relief almost outweighed her embarrassment.

Ryan exhaled harshly, the only sound in the room other than the quiet hum of the air conditioner.

"How long were you awake?"

The brush of his hand against her breast, the touch of his fingers against her nipple, the nudge of his erection between her buttocks—how much had she felt? Phoebe was not a woman given to lying—to herself or to others, overtly or through omission. But facing Ryan with this truth was one of the hardest things she'd ever done.

"Long enough." Phoebe fought the urge to weep

and lifted her chin. "I know this will always stand be-tween us, but it's better than having it stand between us as a secret, a lie of omission. I knew what was going on. And I *wanted* you to touch me."

"I WASN'T ASLEEP, either, Phoebe," Ryan admitted. He could still feel her soft curves against him, smell her, hear her soft moan. "I'm sorry. It's no excuse, but the only thing I can offer is the truth. I've never wanted an-other woman the way I want you."

Phoebe stared at him, her eyes dark and smoky, her breathing unsteady. He closed the gap separating them. She turned her head, looking away from him, her silky braids resting against his face. "What's hap-pening to us, Ryan?"

"The only thing I know for sure is that I want you more than my next breath." He leaned back and traced the line of her jaw with his finger. She quivered at his touch. "I don't know. I didn't wake up and decide to complicate my life by wanting you to the point of mad-ness." His finger trailed against the line of her throat to the slight hollows of her collarbone and settled on the frantic pulse at the base of her neck. "But I do."

She caught his hand in hers, stilling his exploration. "This is madness. Elliott was...just Elliott. I'm fine with what happened. But you're my best friend. I'm closer to you than any other human being. You're my confi-dant. You know me, accept me, warts and all. I can't ruin that by wanting you."

"Do you want me?" He knew the answer, but he

needed to make sure she did. The answer was in her eyes, along with panic. Ryan knew how Phoebe felt about change. A shift of this magnitude would obviously terrify her. Hell, he was even a little thrown off. But she couldn't run from this. "Don't lie to either one of us. Do you want me?"

"Yes." She worried the fullness of her lower lip with her teeth. "Yes, you know I do."

"Phoebe, you're one of the most important people in my life. I don't want to screw that up, either. But pretending I don't ache for you doesn't make it so." He traced the ridge of scar beneath her chin. "This isn't just going to go away if we ignore it. It's a hunger that'll gnaw at us."

She studied his face for a full minute, digesting his words. "All I could think about on the beach today was touching you. Being touched by you." Her words set him on fire. "If we leave things the way they are, the mystique, the temptation, the fantasy will always be there." She paused, then her expression suddenly changed. Ryan knew that look. Phoebe had another plan.

She reached up and started working one of his buttons free. "I think you're right. There's no going back. The only way to deal with this is to move forward," she said as another button gave way. The slide of her fingers against his chest rendered his brain fairly useless. "What we have to do, is to work through this sexual thing between us." Three buttons down. He had no clue how many to go. "You're absolutely right."

Ryan sucked in a deep breath when the back of her fingers skimmed his belly, his entire body vibrating from her touch. "Did I say that?"

She paused. "Didn't you?"

"Does that mean we get to have sex?"

Her fingers lingered above his belt buckle. "Yes, I think it does."

He fell back onto the bed, pulling her on top of him. "Then that's exactly what I said."

PHOEBE WASN'T totally convinced their logic wasn't a bit flawed, skewed perhaps, by lust. But an overwhelming sense of rightness, of destiny was there, as well. And quite frankly she didn't know where else to go with this madness that wasn't going to be resolved by denial.

If they were about to debunk the myth, she wanted to leave no stone unturned to torment herself with "what ifs" later.

She tugged his shirttail free of his pants. "I want to taste you." She leaned forward and pressed nibbling kisses against his stomach, inhaling his male scent.

She dipped her head and traced a path against his naked belly with her tongue, along the waistband of his slacks to the indent of his navel, her beaded braids dragging across his erection. There was more than an element of the forbidden in tasting the slight saltiness of his skin while inhaling his familiar scent. His muscles clenched beneath her mouth. "I love the taste of your skin."

"And I love the way you taste my skin." Ryan said. "I think I'm going to learn a new appreciation for your delayed gratification approach." She moved her head, her beads teasing against his tented trousers. "That is, if you don't kill me first."

Phoebe felt a deeper sense of intimacy and freedom than she'd ever felt with another lover—perhaps because she knew Ryan so well in every other aspect. She laughed softly against the warmth of his midsection as she mapped the contours of hard muscle beneath satin skin with her mouth. She traversed the smooth lines of his side. The pounding of his heart, the echoing rhythm of her own, sounded in her head as she focused on the ridges lightly covered with a smattering of gold-tipped hair. She felt almost drunk from the touch, taste and scent of him.

She flicked her tongue against his flat male nipple and then suckled it. Ryan groaned and closed his eyes. "Oh, baby, that feels so..." She moved to the other nipple, her breasts rubbing against his naked, hair-roughened stomach with exquisite torture. "Yes. Yes." Her body quickened at his appreciation. His obvious pleasure fed hers.

Chest heaving, he impatiently dragged her head up and kissed her, his big hands cupping her head. Phoebe passed the point of rational thought when Ryan suckled her lower lip, then released it and laved his tongue across its swollen surface. He followed the course with his finger, the faint scrape of his callous arousing after the wet velvet of his tongue. "You have the most incredible mouth."

His rough, excited voice scraped along her nerve endings, sending her internal temperature to an incendiary level.

She caught the tip of his finger in her mouth and fondled it with her tongue. His pupils dilated. His eyes darkened. "The better to please you," she teased.

Abruptly, Ryan withdrew his finger and shifted her to her back. "I think we need to elevate your ankle."

Phoebe understood all too well the game of give and take they played. He grabbed a pillow from the head of the bed and propped her ankle on it, the difference in elevation making her legs gape apart.

Ryan paused, his look smoldering as she lay on the bed. She felt wickedly sexy.

He stood, turning his back to her. "Does it feel swollen? Is it throbbing?" His matter-of-fact, almost conversational tone lent the words even more sensual impact. They both knew he wasn't talking about her ankle. He shrugged out of his shirt.

"Yes." She managed to breathe the word. Yes, she was throbbing, swollen. And yes, she wanted to watch him undress.

She finally admitted what she'd denied so long. She'd spent a lifetime looking at the candy bar on the shelf, secretly coveting it. Unaware, until lately, that she wanted it for herself. Now she got to unwrap it. Savor the experience. Even though she knew she didn't need it and inevitably it would prove bad for her in the long run.

Muscles rippled the sculpted line of his back and shoulders as he dropped the shirt to the floor behind him without turning around.

"What are you wearing under that dress? Are you wearing panties, Phoebe? A bra?" He spoke in that same light, vaguely disinterested tone as he pulled his belt through the loops.

Acutely aware of the play of fabric against her hardened nipples, the ride of material between her legs, she shifted on the bed. "No bra. Just panties."

"Really? What kind of panties?" A harsh note flavored his casual question, followed by the sound of a zipper.

"White. A thong." Aroused, she rubbed her palm against the white spandex covering her thighs. Phoebe ached for Ryan's touch.

His entire body stilled. Then he stepped out of his pants. Her breath caught in her throat. He was awesome. Simply awesome. From this angle, everything was tight and hard. Back, buttocks, thighs...

Gripped by intense longing, she instinctively smoothed her dress to the top of her thighs and splayed her legs. "If you want to know what my panties look like, why don't you turn around and see for yourself?"

"If the view gets any better than it is now, I'm not sure I can stand it."

She looked past him. Her eyes locked with his in the

mirror. He'd watched her in the dresser mirror. His tight smile relayed just how much he liked what he saw. Heat threatened to consume her. Emboldened by his obvious turn-on, she dropped her legs wider apart. "And I can't stand it if you don't."

Ryan turned and stood at the foot of the bed. He devoured her with his gaze, a wicked smile revealing his dimple. How many times had she seen him in a bathing suit? His briefs covered the same area. The difference must be the raging erection straining the fabric and the knowledge that before the night was over, she'd have intimate knowledge of what lay beneath.

"You are a goddess."

Phoebe thought about the stubborn cellulite that refused to budge from the backs of her thighs. And then she looked at Ryan, felt the heat of his gaze brush against her skin like a warm balmy breeze, recognized the naked desire in his eyes. He stared at the juncture of her thighs, at the small triangle of material covering her. And, oddly enough, she did feel like a goddess—beautiful and powerful and unfazed by imperfections he didn't seem to see.

"Want to hear a fantasy?" He dropped to the foot of the bed, his voice low, dark. He ran his finger along the top of her foot, the light stroke imbued with an intimacy that shivered through her.

They'd shared so much over the years, but this took it to a new level. "Tell me your fantasy." Need lent a husky quality to her voice.

"Earlier this week, I was on the beach." His fingers

traced the hollows of her ankle. "And I saw a woman with the most incredible legs." He lightly massaged her calf in his big hands, his callouses rasping against her sensitized flesh.

"I didn't know you were a leg man." Phoebe spoke on an indrawn breath. He'd always favored short women with big boobs.

"Neither did I."

"It's good to develop new interests." She dropped her head back. No one had ever stroked her legs with such devastating eroticism.

He gentled her legs farther apart. "This goes far beyond interest." He lowered his head and traced his tongue against the back of her knee, his mouth warm and moist in direct contrast to the scrape of his stubbled jaw.

Phoebe moaned deep in her throat as sensation arced through her. Lying between her legs, he did the same to her other knee. Oh, my. If his mouth felt that good against her knee and she still had all her clothes on... She closed her eyes, savoring the sensation, her muscles clenching, "Yes. That feels so good."

"That's it, baby. Tell me what you like. I want to know." His low, rich voice whispered over her.

She opened her eyes. His broad shoulders filled the narrowing vee of her legs. She skimmed her instep along his waist and over his hip, curling her toes against his tight ass. His muscles flexed against the sole of her foot. "You were telling me about your fantasy," she prompted.

"Hmm. I got distracted." He splayed his fingers on her thighs, his thumbs tracing lazy circles on her inner legs. Phoebe wet her lips as the tension inside her increased. She ached for him to reach higher, past the tops of her thighs.

"So, this woman had these really great, long..." He ran the tip of his tongue from her knee to mid-thigh. She shivered soul deep. "...luscious..." He stroked a wider path up to her inner thigh "...legs."

He raised his head, looking up the length of her body from the juncture of her thighs. His moist breath gusted through the thin scrap of her thong and met her wet, hot flesh. Closing his eyes, he inhaled deeply. "Ah, honey, your scent makes me rock hard."

His comment made her wetter still. "Ryan..." She arched her hips toward him.

He subtly inched back, keeping her needy. He hooked his thumbs beneath the edge of her skirt and tugged it a few inches higher. "I keep getting off the subject." He rested one hand on her panty, just out of reach of where she ached for him. He trailed hot, moist kisses from her inner thigh to the tender skin between her belly and hip, his cheek and jaw brushing maddeningly against her crotch. He nuzzled and nibbled along the edge of her underwear, teasing yet offering no relief to a tension notched so high, she stood poised on the point of shattering.

She wanted—no, needed—more. His mouth. His hand. Something more satisfying than his warm breath and teasing kisses that promised but didn't satisfy.

Driven to the point of distraction, she writhed against him, "Damn your teasing black soul to hell, Ryan Palmer." She sorely resented the fact she was about to fly into a million pieces and he was so in control.

"Oh, baby, we're not hell bound. But I haven't finished telling you my story yet." He tugged her upright. They faced one another, their chests heaving. He reached behind her and found her zipper. "When I saw this fantasy woman on the beach with the legs that made me ache and these sexy, erotic cornrows, all I could imagine—" cool air kissed her back as he slid her zipper down "—was that woman, naked, beneath me," he caressed up the curve of her back and released the button on the neck of her dress, "me buried deep inside her, with those incredible legs wrapped around me." The neck of her dress fell forward, leaving her breasts almost exposed. Ryan leaned back and watched her. "So, what do you think about my fantasy?"

She thought she was bordering on the brink of madness, and she had absolutely no intention of suffering this deprivation alone. He was far too in control of himself. Phoebe caught the end of her dress and slowly pulled it up past her navel, past her breasts and over her head, her movements deliberate, seductive. She tossed the dress to the foot of the bed. "I think fantasy is nice—" she wrapped her legs around his waist and leaned back, bracing herself with her hands behind her "—but reality may be even better."

RYAN DREW a deep, shuddering breath and entertained the notion that reality might, in this instance, with this woman, indeed surpass fantasy. Every other fantasy, had been a dress rehearsal, preparing him for this. For her. This went beyond the physical. They had been an integral part of one another for years. Making love to Phoebe, with Phoebe, was the culmination. The end. And a beginning.

"This reality *is* already better." He ran his fingers along her rib cage, finding pleasure in the tactile smoothness. "Your skin is so soft." His thumbs circled below her breasts, building up the tension for her, for him. Her nipples tightened even more, pouting at puckered attention. Easing his hands around to her back, he pulled her forward and up, circling her delicate tip with his tongue. Ravening hunger surged through him, and he tugged her nipple deeper into his mouth. She pushed her wet heat against his erection, and he pressed against her.

Winding her hands around his neck, she arched her back, thrusting deeper into his mouth with a moan. Ryan readily accommodated her request, moving from one breast to the other. Sensation, emotion swamped him. Everything was thick. The air between them resonated with want, need. The musky scent of their arousal mingled with Phoebe's perfume, hung in the air thick and heavy like the nectar of ripe fruit. His blood coursed, thick with desire. His entire body was caught up in her taste, her scent, her texture and the overwhelming drive to be closer to her, to be a part of her.

Ryan enjoyed sex—sometimes more than others—but this, this was different. This wasn't the mere quest for pleasure. This was an urge that bordered on desperation.

With each tug on her nipple, her sex quivered against his hard-on, dampening his boxers with her arousal. He was burning up. "God. You're so wet and hot." He wrapped his hand around the back of her thong and tugged, pulling the material tight against her. "Do you like this?"

She ground against him, her breath coming in short, sharp pants, her hands clenching hard into his shoulders. "Yes. Yes, I like it. What about you?" She reached between them and pulled his rigid erection through the opening of his shorts. "Do you like it when I touch you like this?" She closed her hand around his length and stroked.

Ryan drew in a sharp breath. "Yes. I like it when you touch me like that."

She tugged his mouth down to hers, her sherry eyes glittering with hot arousal and wanton intent. She kissed him openmouthed, her tongue stroking in time with her hand. Stroke by stroke, she melted the glue holding him together. Frantic for more, he buried his hands in the mounds of her bottom, urging her slick, wet heat closer. Just at the point when he thought he would explode, her hand stilled and she wrenched her mouth away from his.

"Ryan. If we don't do this soon, I'm going to lose my mind."

It was a request and a warning.

"Baby, I've already lost my mind." He began to ease her onto her back. She stilled him with a hand to his chest.

"No. Stay just like that."

"Okay." Hell, at this point she could tell him to get down on all fours and bark like a dog and he'd willingly howl at the moon. He was pretty damn close to howling right now.

With a supple twist of her hips, she raised up and tugged her thong aside. "Now, let's go slow."

Ryan grasped her hips and eased her onto his erection. Her legs still wrapped around his waist, she sank down on him with excruciating slowness. Inch by inch, she wrapped her wet heat around him. Ryan closed his eyes, flooded by pleasure as he entered her tight, hot paradise.

For a moment they both held absolutely still as she settled against him, joined as fully and deeply as possible. With no outward sign of movement, she clenched her muscles around him, deep inside her.

"Oh, Phoebe, baby."

She dropped her head back. "Yes. You feel so good." She clenched again, and he pulsed a response. Her nipples stabbed against the wall of his chest, and he cupped her braided head in his hands and kissed her, hard, deep. And then she began a rocking, grinding motion against him, her muscles gripping him, milking him. Unable to thrust in that position, he ground against her in response, picking up her rhythm.

He was so close to coming but he gritted his teeth and held himself in check, unwilling to go there without Phoebe. He felt spasms begin to radiate from her core. "That's it, Phoebe. Let it go, baby."

As they both found a release, Ryan realized what a hollow experience sex had been before. Nothing more than a physical release. Nothing close to the richness of sharing your body with a woman so intimately acquainted with your mind.

They collapsed against the mattress, still joined. Sated, he could stay inside her forever.

Every fantasy he'd ever had paled in comparison to this moment.

7

PHOEBE'S EYES drifted shut. Emotions, thoughts stirred and blew though her like gossamer fabric fluttering in the breeze. Complete. Replete. Making love with Ryan had brought a pleasure, a completeness so clear and pure, it evoked a piercing melancholy.

She absorbed the texture of his skin against hers, the heat of his hair-sprinkled belly, the fine coating of sweat that slicked them both, the fragrant musk produced by their union.

With startling clarity, Phoebe realized she'd always withheld something of herself during lovemaking. An emotional reserve. A part of her that was hers alone, a part of herself she was unwilling to share. Participation without full engagement. But with Ryan, there'd been no holding back. It hadn't been a conscious decision, it had just happened. She'd given all of herself. In return, she'd realized gratification she'd never known before.

Next to her, Ryan moved, his fingers playing along the line of her hip, his breath warm against her cooling neck. "You asleep, Phoebes?"

"No." Eyes still closed, she smoothed her foot against his calf, enjoying the tactile play of hair and muscle against her arch. One last time. Phoebe opened her eyes, reluctant to deal with the practicalities of their relationship quite so soon. Knowing, however, that she couldn't languish in the aftermath of lovemaking forever. She shifted her leg off his. "No. I'm not asleep."

He dragged his fingers across her stomach, as if he, too, was reluctant to give up the contact. God, they'd just made everything worse. They'd debunked nothing except their own foolishness.

Rolling to the other side, Phoebe put the width of the king-size mattress between them. She tugged the edge of the comforter over her, suddenly self-consciously aware of her near nudity. Thongs didn't count for much in the coverage department. "Yep. Good thing we got that over with." Awkwardness, the aftermath of spent passion and uncertainty in how to proceed, settled between them.

"So, what do you—"

"Want to—"

They both laughed, rounding off the sharp edge of tension. Phoebe made the mistake of looking at him. All of him. Splendidly, rousingly naked. Ryan wasn't just a hottie. He was a one-man, twelve-alarm fire waiting to happen. Even now, her body stirred in response to his nudity and proximity. And that wasn't part of her plan. She'd figured that making love once would dispel the mystique. Only it hadn't. What a disaster. Phoebe trained her eyes on his face, determined to look no farther south than his neck. "Go ahead."

"No. You first."

"You. I insist."

"Okay." Ryan shrugged, and Phoebe swallowed hard. Amazing, really, how many well-honed, sleek muscles tightened and rippled and generally put on a sensual show when a naked man shrugged. "I was going to ask if you were ready to go to bed?" A banked fire smoldered in his eyes.

"Here?" Phoebe closed her eyes, envisioning them wrapped in each other's arms. "Of course you mean here." The idea of crawling beneath the sheets with Ryan, his smell and taste still imprinted on her, didn't seem such a clever idea. She shook her head. "I don't think so. I'm really not tired. In fact, I'm pretty energized."

While she spoke, she employed a few contortionist moves, trying to retrieve her dress from where it lay wedged between the bottom corner post and the mattress while keeping the comforter wrapped around her. "But you go to bed if you want to. I'll be really quiet. You won't even know I'm here."

Ryan looked at her, his eyes caressing the swell of her breasts above the comforter, a predatory smile tugging at his mouth. "I'd give it about a snowball's chance in hell that I won't know you're around."

Her hand holding the comforter in place shook. And damnation if her nipples didn't peak to hard buds just at his hot glance and suggestive smile. What had she been thinking to get herself in this position with her best friend and playboy extraordinaire?

"Oh." How else was she supposed to respond? It

was either that or jumping his bones again, and more bone-jumping wasn't an option.

"Let me help." Ryan reached down and tugged, his head far too near her comforter-covered breasts for her peace of mind. He worked the dress free. "Here."

Instead of the width of the bed, mere inches separated them. Ryan stared at her mouth. Her lower lip tingled from his gaze, as if he'd actually brushed her mouth with his. He held her dress in his fist.

"Ryan..." His name lingered against her tongue.

"Phoebe...." He dropped his head forward, so close she could see the bristles that cast a golden shadow over his jaw, feel the heat of his body. An answering heat unfurled through her like a ribbon slowly coming undone.

This was all wrong. They'd made love once. That should have taken care of this yearning inside her. Frustration welled. She wanted him as much or more than she had before

God, she would be lost if she didn't put a stop to this madness right now. "I need my dress, Ryan."

"Sure." He handed her the dress but otherwise didn't move.

Phoebe shoved it under her armpits, stretching it across her breasts like a giant Band-Aid. She backed off the side of the bed with all the poise of a sand crab scuttling for cover. "Okay, then. I'm just going to put on my bathing suit and go for a swim."

She backed across the room to the bathroom. Not too terribly dignified, but then neither was turning around and showing off her cellulite depository. Yeah, she'd been on the beach in a bathing suit, but you just sort of hoped nobody looked too close. That was a far different proposition than turning around and flashing the best friend you just had incredible, once-in-a-lifetime sex with.

"What are you doing, Phoebe?"

Was that a note of exasperation? "I just told you, I'm going to pop in here and put on my bathing suit."

"But why are you backing across the room?"

Now she was feeling altogether foolish and awkward. Why wouldn't he just drop it?

"The, uh, you know...I'm only wearing the butt floss." Infuriated at finding herself in this position, she yelled the last part.

"I've seen you naked, Phoebe," Ryan shouted. "Well, almost naked, except for that butt floss, which is seriously sexy, by the way."

Reaching behind her, Phoebe awkwardly opened the door and edged into the bathroom. "Yeah. Well, I've seen you naked, too." And that was seriously sexy, also. She slammed the door and clicked the lock into place for good measure.

She'd seen him, felt him, heard him, tasted him, smelled him—she'd had the total sensory experience. And therein lay the crux of the whole problem. She wasn't likely to forget it anytime soon.

THIS WAS ridiculous. Ryan pulled on his swimming trunks. He and Phoebe yelling at one another. Then not speaking when she flounced through the room on the way to the pool. And now she was out in that little round pool that was essentially made for lounging and aqua sex, swimming circular laps so fast she was probably dizzy.

He snatched the bucket of iced champagne and two glasses that came with the suite. For all the years he'd known Phoebe, he realized he didn't have a clue as to what was going on in her sexy head right now. But he damn sure intended to find out.

He shouldered the door open, then stepped onto the walled patio, dark except for the moonlight filtering through palms and the swath of light from the French door, still ajar. Phoebe had abandoned her circular laps and floated on her back, her braids spread on the water around her.

"Go away," she ordered without opening her eyes.

"No." He put the champagne bucket and glasses on the tile and slipped into the pool. "We're going to talk."

"I don't want to talk."

"Too bad. I can sit here all night if that's what it takes." What? Did she think she was the only one involved here? The last time he'd checked, he was the other half of the equation. He uncorked the bottle and poured two glasses.

"You are so obstinate."

"Yep. Now there's a nice glass of Cordon Negro waiting on you over here whenever you decide you're ready."

Phoebe crossed the pool, shooting him a mutinous look. She reached for her champagne. "So, talk."

"Why are you angry with me?"

"I'm not."

"Then why'd you yell?"

"You yelled back." She took another sip.

"Phoebe, this isn't getting us anywhere."

"Okay. I yelled because I'm so frustrated I could scream. And yelling seemed a marginally better choice than screaming."

"Frustrated? But I thought...you seemed to enjoy it."

"That's the problem. I did enjoy it."

"Okay." She was pissed because the sex had been too good. That was a first. Actually, it hadn't been just good—it had been incredible. Stupendous. Just thinking about it, he began to thicken, harden.

She upended her champagne glass and held it out for a refill. She rested her head against the side of the pool and looked at the half-moon, a woeful expression on her face. "You know, if it had been lousy, it would've been embarrassing, but we could've just written it off to bad chemistry. Mediocre chemistry." She paused long enough to swig her champagne. "But no. It's spectacular. The best sex of my life, and it has to be with you."

"You wanted to have bad sex?" On a good day, the workings of the female mind were convoluted and somewhat mysterious, which often made it very interesting to have a best friend who was a woman. Except half the time, Phoebe thought like a guy. At least he thought she did. Guys never hoped for bad sex—it just happened sometimes. Nonetheless, he struggled to grasp her point. "So, you're mad because the sex was so good with us?"

"The plan was to sleep together so we could get past it. But it only made it worse than ever. How can I ever be around you without remembering how good it was? Not any time in the foreseeable future, I can assure you." She turned her back to him, propping her crossed arms and chin on the side of the pool.

Moonlight danced across the curves of her back, leaving hollows and indentions he longed to explore. His pulse hammered an acknowledgment. "I know what you mean."

She glanced over her shoulder, "You do?"

Her taste. Her scent. The feel of her clenching around him while he was buried deep inside her. Making love with her had only whetted his appetite. "I definitely won't forget what it was like with you anytime soon, either."

PHOEBE LOOKED away, a new plan forming in her mind, one born of desperation, an out-of-control sex drive, moonlight and two, maybe three glasses of Cordon Negro. There, she'd blamed just about every factor she could. "You know it couldn't possibly be that good between us again."

She didn't have to turn her head to know he was behind her. She felt his nearness in the shiver that chased down her spine. "It doesn't seem likely, does it?" he responded.

Her heart thundered as she gave voice to her madness. "Probably just a fluke. If we had the courage to try it again, it'd probably be terrible. A real disappointment."

Ryan wrapped his arms around her bare midriff, pulling her against him. Like a match to tinder, heat raced through her. "I'm willing to give it a second try if you are."

His mouth, warm and wet, nuzzled her shoulder and the sensitive skin on the side of her neck. All she could think about was the feel of his mouth on her and the ache to have him inside her once again. She dropped her head to his shoulder, allowing him more thorough access.

"Do you want me to touch you?" His voice, low and rough, raked across her nerve endings. The rigid, thick line of his erection nudged its way between her buttocks. Instinctively she wiggled closer. "Tell me, Phoebe. Let me hear it."

"Yes. Yes. Please." Her voice was ragged with need.

He reached up and slid his hands beneath her bikini top. She clasped his forearms, urging him on. He cupped her breasts in his hands, massaging the undersides, weighing their fullness. She arched against him, desperate for his touch, for the release from the sweet torment plaguing her. Finally, he reached up and touched her nipples. Her entire body convulsed as he alternated smoothing, plucking and rolling her turgid points between his fingertips. She moaned into the night and ground her buttocks against him.

The scents of champagne and Ryan enveloped her as he nibbled at the lobe of her ear. The scrape of his jaw against her neck sent chills skittering across her skin. It was arousing beyond anything she'd ever imagined, the sensation of cool water and chills on the outside while a white-hot heat licked at her inside.

"It's going to be good, again, isn't it?" Anticipation and dread heightened her excitement.

"It feels like it, baby." His heartbeat hammered against her back, his breath harsh in her ear.

She was already wound so tight and ready for him she teetered on the verge of disintegrating. She whispered over her shoulder, low and urgent. "Now, Ryan. I want you now. Like this."

She snatched at her bikini top and skimmed off her bottoms, leaning forward to drag them off.

Ryan groaned as she bent in the water in front of him. "Like this?"

She looked over her shoulder as she pulled her bottoms off one foot. "Yes. Like this."

Moonlight illuminated his face. Desire etched his features and corded his muscles. He devoured her with his eyes while he took off his swimming trunks. Aching for him to fill her, she turned her back to him and grasped the edge of the pool.

His big hands wrapped around her hips. Eager. Urgent. She pushed back against his erection, spreading her legs. With one decisive thrust he filled her. Sweet. Brimming.

His thrusts rendered languid by the water, it was like making love in slow motion. She quivered, gloriously tuned in to each nuance, the weight of her braids against her neck, Ryan's hands gripping her hips, the thick length of him deep within her, the hard wall of his thighs behind her. Ryan laid claim to her with the phrases of a lover. She answered him, whispered snatches of broken words floating in the night air.

Tiny tremors radiated from her core, building in intensity with each plunge. Just as before, there was no holding back. A maelstrom of emotion built inside her along with the physical sensations.

A low keening unfurled from within and rose from her throat as Ryan shuddered within her, matching and urging on the tremors that racked her as they fused and became one.

Ryan sank onto the built-in seat, pulling her down on his lap, his arms wrapped around her. Exhausted and precariously close to incoherent, she settled there, her cheek finding comfort in the solid plane of his chest.

They sat for what could have been hours, minutes, seconds, a lifetime. The cool water soothed them until their breathing slowed and their heartbeats calmed to something close to normal. Phoebe tasted wet salt and realized it was the brine of her tears trickling down her face. She sniffed, desperately trying to suck them up.

Ryan pulled her closer, pressing a kiss to the top of her head.

"Phoebe, honey, why are you crying?" His palm moved against her back in soothing small circles. "Please don't cry, baby. It's going to be okay."

She snuffled against the warm satin of his skin, her tears mingling with the droplets of water caught in his chest hair. She swiped at her eyes and leaned against his shoulder. She couldn't speak past the knot of tears lodged in her throat.

"It'll be all right."

Moonlight gilded his hair to a molten gold. His face reflected an intense tenderness. God, he was so dear to her. He'd been such an important part of her life. Panic clutched at her. What if this destroyed them? "But what if it's not? What if things are never okay with us again?"

Ryan's mouth found hers. His lips offered comfort and reassurance and she readily took what he offered, his kiss calming her panic. As he started to pull away, his lips lingered a second too long, and Phoebe sensed the shadow of lurking desire.

She pulled away, resting her back against his arm. "Rank the first time tonight on a scale of one to ten."

"I don't think we should do that, Phoebe. It really goes against the grain." He idly toyed with one of her braids, rolling it between his fingers.

"Well, pretend it wasn't me. I mean, not the me you made love to, but the me that's your friend."

Ryan's brows met in a dubious frown.

"Say I was some strange woman you picked up on the beach and had sex with."

"This might be easier to do if you weren't sitting on my lap while we're both naked. You know if you're going to be sitting there and we're talking about this..." He stirred against her hip.

Oh, my God. "Twice in one night? You can't—" She stumbled to a halt.

"Well, hell, Phoebe, you don't have to make me sound like a freak. It seems to have a mind of its own, and you have that effect on it."

Hovering somewhere between gratification and mortification, Phoebe moved to the opposite corner. As far away from Ryan as possible.

"Okay. I met this gorgeous stranger on the beach and had some of the best sex of my life." Only *some* of the best sex? Phoebe tried not to scowl. That should be good news. Ryan changed the subject. "Do you do this with other men? Rank the performance—cause I've got to tell you, it's a bad idea."

Ryan paused, then said, "Okay. On a scale of one to ten? I'd give it a twelve."

"Of course I don't do this with other men. But this is you. Twelve? Okay. I'd go with a twelve myself. What about just now? A few minutes ago?" Just thinking about a few minutes ago left her hot and needy.

"You're not going to want to hear this." Latent arousal threaded his voice.

"Probably not." She steeled herself. "Go ahead."

Ryan drew a deep breath and huffed it out. "The best sex of my life. At least a thirteen and a half."

"Damnation." They were sunk. Goners.

"I know. What about you?"

"I'd give it a solid fourteen, myself." She rested her arms along the back of the pool and leaned her head against the smooth inlaid pebbles, looking to the star-sprinkled sky for inspiration, determined not to panic over jeopardizing the most important relationship in her life. "We've got to come up with a plan. Plans A and B have been disasters. Any ideas?"

Except for the distant revelry of partygoers, the faint crash of waves breaking on the shore and the steady flow of water circulating in the mini waterfall, the night was quiet. Although the sky was beautiful, radiant with stars, it didn't offer any fast solution. Neither did Ryan, for that matter. He better not have fallen asleep.

"Ryan?" She lifted her head.

He wasn't asleep. Phoebe realized she'd scooted up, leaving her breasts half out of the water, her nipples barely covered. The lover in her wanted to slide up and revel in the caressing heat of his gaze. The friend in her wanted to sink lower. She sat stock-still, incapable of either.

"Ryan..." She paused and cleared her throat. That low husky voice that resonated like a lover's plea wouldn't do at all. "Ryan..." Yes, that was much better, stronger, firmer. "We need a plan."

"A plan? Can't we just see what happens?"

"I can't do that. You know I can't." She drank in the sight of him across the moonlight-dappled water, her heart contracting.

"Then we'll come up with a plan," her friend promised.

8

SWEATING FROM an early morning run, Phoebe slipped the room card into the door. The empty beach and fresh morning sky, coupled with a long run, had given her a new perspective. Things had been crazy. Both of them had been caught up in the sensual magic of the island. But today was a new day. She'd take a nice hot shower and then she and her best friend would have breakfast and come up with a new plan. Today things would be back to normal with Ryan.

She felt upbeat, resolute. Until she walked in the door and Ryan walked out of the bathroom, wearing nothing but sexy, low-slung pajama bottoms and a smile, a towel thrown around his neck.

"How was your run?" He brushed his hand through his hair, his stomach muscles rippling with the movement. A general flutter started low in her belly, dangerously close to shooting her resolve to hell.

"Good. I'm sweaty so I'm just going to hop in the shower." She would ignore this breathless longing and treat him like a friend. She brushed past him, but he followed her into the sumptuous bathroom.

"I said I was going to take a shower," she reminded him.

"I was just about to shave. Do you mind if I shave while you shower?" There was a challenge there, to see if they could get back to a nonsexual footing.

The sane, rational side of her protested that it was a very bad idea. The competitive side of her challenged her to put her money where her mouth was and treat him like a friend.

"That shouldn't be a problem. Just let me get in first." She could do this. She walked over and turned on the water to let it heat up.

She unlaced her running shoes and took them off. It was far more productive than ogling his bare chest. Except it put her at eye level with his naked belly and pajama-clad groin. She straightened abruptly, biting back a sigh.

Phoebe peeled off her socks, careful not to bend down this time.

She tried to ignore the frisson of desire that clutched at her. "Turn around so I can undress."

The air thickened with wet, hot steam, stirred by a provocative awareness that threatened all her clear-headed resolutions.

Ryan turned. His back offered a study in symmetry and grace. The thin cotton of his pajamas outlined his tight butt.

Phoebe stripped, ran to the shower and stepped beneath the stinging spray.

"Are you in?"

"Yes."

"How's the water?"

"Fine."

Phoebe desperately tried to recall some gross, disgusting fact about Ryan to offset her general state of extreme arousal. Unfortunately, nothing came to mind except how very erotic it was, talking to Ryan's bare back while warm water sluiced over her shoulders and streamed down her back, the curve of her buttocks, the length of her legs. Was she destined to spend this entire trip wet, in some fashion or another, and naked or nearly thereabouts?

The best course of action, at this point, was to get the shower over. A quick wash and she'd be done. She looked around for the soap. Great. She was in the shower. The soap was on the sink, next to Ryan. "Would you hand me the soap? Please?"

"Do you need anything else?" His suggestion, low and husky, unleashed all the memories of last night's lovemaking.

"Just the soap."

He handed it around the glass door, taking care not to look. Her fingers brushed his as she took it from him, the simple contact arrowing through her, tightening her nipples to hard points.

"Thanks."

Frustration, exasperation and more than a little confusion welled inside her. She felt the foundation of their friendship shifting before her very eyes, undermined by the attraction throbbing between them. Even now, in the silence that stretched between them, though they were separated by the glass of the shower stall, a thread of sexual tension connected them as surely as if it were woven into the fabric of her being.

Craving sensitized her skin. She sucked in a breath as she dragged the washcloth across her shoulders. Tension coiled inside her. Tight, hot, wet tension.

"Phoebe, this isn't working."

"It's not?"

"No. You in there, naked and wet. Me out here."

How did he know she was wet? Oh, yeah. The shower. "But..."

Ryan pivoted in slow motion. Phoebe stopped in midsentence. Longing etched his face. Through the shower glass, his eyes devoured her. "I want you so badly, I hurt."

The pounding of her heart sounded in her head with the pounding of the water. God, she was swimming upstream, fighting the current of sexual need that threatened to sweep her away. And quite frankly, she didn't know if she could find her way back to where she'd begun. Right now, she was in desperate danger of drowning.

She opened the shower door tugged him in, tired of fighting the current, latching on to him as if he alone could save her. Ryan stepped inside, pajama bottoms and all, his mouth latching onto hers, driving her through the spray until her back and buttocks pressed against the marble wall. She surged into him, desperate to be close to him.

"Oh, Phoebe," he moaned against her mouth, as if he shared her desperation. He captured her wrists in his left hand and raised them over her head, holding them against the wall, pinning her there. It was an erotically vulnerable position that demanded a level of trust. Water cascaded around them, between them, spraying her face, stinging her eyes. He picked up the bar of soap and massaged it in one hand until creamy, white foam dripped from his fingers. The bar dropped to the shower floor with a dull thunk.

Phoebe's breath came in short, hard pants. Anticipation of his touch bowed her body. With exquisite care, he smoothed his soap-slicked fingers down her neck, along her collarbone. Instead of satisfying, his touch fed the hunger that gripped her.

He stroked the hollow of her armpit and she trembled. Her armpit? Good God, she was in serious trouble if he could make her armpit feel good. And he did.

His clever, nimble fingers smoothed down to the fleshy outside of her breast. He lathered the soft underside, his fingers rubbing the crease where gravity had taken its toll. Her nipples tightened and puckered eagerly against the spray, awaiting his touch. His palm smoothed her peak, his touch echoing through her body.

Phoebe closed her eyes and dropped her head against the marble, giving herself over to the sensations drenching her. He mirrored his ministrations on her right side then moved lower, soaping the indentation of her waist, the expanse of her stomach.

"You have the sexiest belly." His finger rimmed and

dipped into her navel while he held her wrists captive above her head with his other hand.

It should've been a position of enslavement. It was a position of power, evident in the tremble of his hand, the hoarse note in his voice, the intense heat in his eyes.

He slid his hand to the rounded line of her hips. Instinctively, she shifted her feet wider apart, opening herself to him. Ryan stroked her inner thighs, the back of his fingers brushing against her curls. She couldn't still the moan that floated out into the steam and warm spray. If he'd just move his hand...

"Turn around and let me get your back."

She opened her eyes. He was killing her, touch by touch. "But..."

"All in due time. Be patient. Do you trust me?"

"Yes. I trust you."

"Are your arms tired?"

"No." At any time she could have dropped them if she wanted to. They both knew that. "I like it."

"So do I. Now turn around."

She turned, pressing her cheek and the length of her soaped torso against the wall. She bit her lip as her aroused body pressed against the unyielding marble. Steamy. Slick. Slippery. Wet. Hard.

He massaged and stroked the line of her back, the tight, tense muscles of her shoulders. Each touch, soothing and gentle, coiled the spring inside her tighter still.

She ground against the slick marble when he rotated his thumb down the line of her spine. He cupped and kneaded her too-plump cheeks. His obvious pleasure in her body quieted any lingering self-consciousness. There was no room in this place, with the two of them, for that. Aching for the touch he deliberately withheld, she brought her bottom closer to his hand, bracing her feet farther apart. His fingers intimately delved the margin of her buttocks, pushing her past the point of reason.

She clutched at the marble, sobbing against the wall. Finally, he reached between her legs, separating her folds with two fingers. One stroke. Feather light. His slippery finger against her slick moisture. She shuddered. Her entire body convulsed at the one touch. But it wasn't enough.

He released her wrists. "Stay where you are."

She waited for what was only seconds but could have been hours, racked against the wall with anticipation. He knelt behind her, squeezing her buttocks, separating her.

"I want to taste you, Phoebe." And then his tongue stroked the same path his finger had earlier.

Falling. Soaring. Drowning. Swimming.

"Delicious."

"Ryan...please...don't...stop," she cried against the wall.

His mouth plied her intimately. Lips. Tongue. Stroking. Nibbling. Suckling. Thrusting.

Appeasement of her flesh. Succor to her soul. Relentless pleasure flooded her. Gripped her. Shook her. Seared her.

She slid down the wall, his strong arms banding around her, supporting her.

"That's it, baby. I've got you. Just relax."

Like a marionette without a master, she folded to the shower floor between his legs, spent. Ryan shifted from kneeling to sitting, his back against the other wall, and tugged Phoebe's limp form between his thighs. Warm water surrounded them like a tropical downpour. With his arms wrapped around her from behind, Ryan pulled her against the solid wall of his chest. His hands cupped her breasts, lifting them, the water sluicing away any remnants of soap, the deluge pelting her sensitized nipples. Through the thin soaked cotton of his pajama bottoms, his erection pressed against her.

She leaned back, her head nestled against his shoulder. Content to languish in the warm water, the satisfaction and his solid strength.

"You're incredible, Phoebe. So hot. So sexy. So sweet." She turned her head and Ryan's mouth—warm, wet, musky—moved over hers. Something deep inside her stirred, something beyond physical, although there was that, too.

Maybe she was a deviant. She must be. Because the better the sex, the more she wanted it. The more satisfying, the more short-lived the satisfaction. She'd just experienced one of the most satisfying orgasms of her life, and now she felt the tingle of desire awakening yet again. She knew she couldn't keep falling into these situations with Ryan. But she wanted to give him the same bone-melting, mind-numbing, soul-shattering pleasure he'd given her.

She reached between them and touched him through his sodden pajamas. "I think you could benefit from a little shower therapy."

"Sounds interesting." His eyes glittered as he moved against her hand.

"I think you'll be very pleased." She sat forward and twisted out of his arms, kneeling, the water hitting her back, spray bouncing off her shoulders. "But to realize the full benefit, you need to let me help you out of your pajamas."

Ryan started to stand. Phoebe pushed him back down. "Stay where you are. Just lift your hips."

She rolled the wet cloth over his hips, his hard-on snagging the cloth like a tent pole. Phoebe laughed. Ryan grimaced, laughing as well. "Go ahead. You know what happens when a beautiful woman laughs at a naked man?"

Phoebe laughed again. She dipped her hand beneath the waist of his pajamas and skimmed up the velvet-smooth, rigid length of him. Her breath caught in her throat and her pulse raced as she freed him from the cloth, her smirk fading. "Now you're truly naked. And I assure you—" her finger traced the length of him "—I'm not laughing."

His eyes darkened with arousal. "Neither am I."

She tugged his pyjama down the muscular length of his legs and shoved them into a corner. Turning to the matter at hand, she snagged the soap and worked up a rich lather.

Phoebe straddled his thigh and ran her hands over his shoulders. Hard muscles flexed beneath fine-textured skin. "Touching you is such a pleasure."

"Honey, feel free to pleasure yourself for as long as you like."

Phoebe knew from the odd occasion she'd treated herself to a manicure how good a quick forearm and hand massage felt. She stroked and kneaded his upper arm, his forearm and finally his hand.

"Damn, that feels good. You've got magic hands, Phoebe. I never knew you could do this." Steam swirled around them. Droplets caught in the water-darkened sweep of his lashes.

"Then I guess, I'm doing it right." She smiled at his blissful expression.

"Yeah. I guess you are."

"There are a whole lot of things I know how to do well that you don't know about."

"Now *that's* something to look forward to."

Feeling more sure of herself, she moved to the other arm and then up to his chest.

Leaning forward, he captured her nipple in his mouth and sucked. Hard. She clung to his shoulders and drew a sharp breath as the sensation arrowed straight to her womb. Still holding her in his mouth, he ravished the distended point. "Yes..." she breathed into the swirling steam.

He released her and he dropped his head back.

"And that is one of the pleasures of having a naked woman bathe you."

She angled her other pouting crest close to his mouth. "And here's the second one."

Obligingly, he drew her nipple deep into his mouth, tugging, his teeth scraping lightly against her tip, the sensation reminiscent of his mouth on her earlier. Oh, God. She closed her eyes. Her low moan bounced off the shower walls.

Ryan released her and she slowly opened her eyes, drawing back. She ran her slick fingers over his flat male nipples. "I think you'll find the benefits get better and better."

"I hope I live that long 'cause baby, you are killing me."

She palmed the flat plane of his belly with small, concentric circles. Sweeping wide, she delicately massaged the flesh flanking his groin. The closer her hands came to his straining hard-on without touching it, the sharper and shorter his breath was. His excitement fed hers, and she quivered along with him when her hands rubbed the clenched muscles of his inner thigh.

She slid out of the range of the spraying water and allowed it to rinse him. She watched him through the torrent. "You'd like for me to touch you, wouldn't you?"

He couldn't want it any more than she did. He breathed harder still, his erection pulsing at her throaty suggestion. "Yes. I would like that very much." His voice echoed with raw need.

Until that moment, Phoebe had planned to touch him. He had taken her to the other side of paradise. She wanted to please him to that same extent.

Phoebe approached him on hands and knees. Water pounded the back of her head, her shoulders. She delicately stroked him from tip to base and cupped him . He closed his eyes and clenched his teeth. "Oh, Phoebe. Oh, baby."

Leaning forward, she probed his tip with her tongue, thoroughly aroused, as wet as he was hard.

His eyes flew open.

"I like touching you, Ryan. But what I really want to do is taste you." She licked up the length of him, pausing at the top. "As long as you know we're not playing basketball and there's no slam-dunking."

She poised, ready to take the length of him in her mouth.

Ryan braced his hands on the shower floor, a hot, sexy smile on his face. "I don't even like basketball."

9

"THE BEACH is crowded," Ryan observed from the table they'd dined at the previous morning. Had it only been twenty-four hours? So much had changed between them, it could have been a lifetime.

Martin poured cups of steaming coffee, and once again they shared an assortment of fruits and a pastry. Ryan watched the snorkeling boat pull away in the distance. Making love to Phoebe had been like snorkeling. It had revealed a whole new facet of her, full of beauty and mystique to discover and share. He was unabashedly enchanted.

She speared a mango chunk. "I can't think about the beach. We've got to come up with a plan."

Thank goodness she'd abandoned the denial plan she'd walked through the door with this morning.

She bit into the ripe fruit. Juice trickled down her chin.

Ryan leaned in and caught the juice with his finger. The texture of her skin against his fingertip was fine and silky. "Ryan..."

Heat shimmered and danced between them, through them, provoked by memories of the morning.

The shower. The steam. Her hands. Her mouth. Release. Pleasure.

"I know." Hell, yes, he knew.

Ryan drank his coffee, savoring the smooth, rich flavor.

Focus. He needed to focus. And not on her sexy, full mouth. He'd promised to help her come up with a plan and he would. When he could think clearly.

"How did this happen to us?" She'd asked it before, but it still confounded her.

Ryan didn't answer immediately.

He glanced up soberly. He hated the distress in her voice. Unlike him, Phoebe required to know *why* before she could accept any situation. "I don't know, Phoebes. Maybe it's this place. The sun is brighter, the sand whiter, the water clearer, the food spicier. Everything is more intense."

"You're more intense," she noted.

Ryan knew it. Felt it. Lovemaking with Phoebe had shifted something inside him. He'd found more than physical release with her. She was frightened by the changes between them. Things had changed so quickly, so completely. Her insistence on a plan clearly reflected her need to clutch at something familiar in the midst of all the changes.

He sliced a section of *pain au chocolat* and pushed the plate to her. If he didn't push her to enjoy at least a mouthful, she'd want it but never touch it .

She bit into the flaky pastry. "Maybe you're right. It must be Jamaica." She paused in sublime appreciation.

"This is sinfully good. It's so rich I only want a few bites." She paused and snapped her fingers. Relief and excitement chased the desperation off her face. "I've got it. I've got the plan. This thing with us, it's like starting a diet."

"I'm not following you." He supposed it was the creativity that made her so successful at her job, but sometimes her convoluted thought processes confounded him.

"You start a diet. The last thing you need is a chocolate-covered doughnut. But the thing you want more than anything is a chocolate-covered doughnut." She waved her hands for emphasis. "You don't even have to close your eyes and you can taste it. Five seconds in the microwave and it's hot and gooey sweet and the chocolate all but melts against your tongue." Her voice slowed, taking on a hoarse quality.

Ryan's body stirred in response. Her words and her slow, husky drawl had sent him to the edge. He didn't have to close his eyes to recall her hot sweetness melting against his tongue.

"Baby, I hope you get to the point pretty damn quick, cause you've already got me to one."

She drew a deep breath. The look in her eyes told him she was remembering the same thing he was. "Stay with me and I'll explain. You have one chocolate-covered doughnut and it's so good, that's all you can think about. How good it was and how you absolutely shouldn't have another one."

"But you want another one." Just like their first time.

"Exactly. Like every time we make love."

Just hearing her talk about their lovemaking aroused him. He'd never wanted a woman so fiercely, so completely before.

"So, what's the solution?"

"Before you start a diet, you buy a dozen doughnuts and you eat them all. The first one's great, the second one's still yummy. The third one is pretty darn good. But the fourth one is just okay. By the time you're up to the tenth one, you either don't want another one or they've gotten stale. See what I mean?"

"You frighten me when you use female logic." However, having unlimited sex beat the hell out of her previous denial plan.

Her provocative smile knocked him for a loop. "Good. You frighten me when you act like the superior male."

He reached for her hand, twining his fingers through hers. Her fingers, like her gorgeous legs, were long and slender. And when they wrapped around him... "Let me make sure I understand. You're suggesting we gorge ourselves on sex with each other?"

"Exactly. Between now and when we leave." Her fingers tightened around his. Her lips parted.

"I think it's a damn shame we're in a public place. Otherwise, I'd show you just how much I like your plan by implementing it immediately." He pressed his lips against the delicate blue vein on the back of her slender hand.

"I'm glad you like it." Her breath quickened.

"I don't usually go in for obsessive-compulsive behavior, but for sex with you I'll make an exception. However, I do have one question."

He nuzzled the fine bones of her wrist, her pulse beating like a wild bird against his mouth.

"Hmm?"

Doughnut theory or not, he couldn't imagine a time when he wouldn't want her again. He knew for damn sure that four more days of intimacy with her wouldn't begin to be enough. He didn't think Phoebe was ready to hear that. She had to move one step at a time.

"Why are you so intent on burning this out with us, Phoebe? Why does this have to end when we leave? Why can't we just see where it goes?"

She toyed with a piece of fruit. "Because this needs to end while we're still friends." She looked at him. "Because we both know this won't last."

"How do you—"

"Because the longest you ever dated one person was four weeks." The specter of his past, all the casual, short-lived relationships, stared at him from the depths of her eyes. "At least this way, neither one of us is sitting around waiting for the shoe to drop." Her voice wavered. "Because our friendship means everything to me."

"But we can..."

She reached over and quieted him with her finger against his lips. "No. Don't say it. Don't even go there. I won't forsake our friendship for a fleeting physical relationship. And joining the Ryan Palmer harem isn't an option.''

A lesser man might have been offended, he reasoned wryly. But at least he knew where he stood with her.

PHOEBE HUNG the Do Not Disturb sign outside their door then closed the door. Anticipation strummed through her. Their days had taken on a pattern. A delicious, addictive, hedonistic pattern. Making love in the morning. A mid-morning excursion or water sport. Back to the privacy of their room for a siesta. Perhaps an afternoon activity. Dinner. And then the long tropical nights.

In the last three days they'd windsurfed, snorkeled, visited Prospect Plantation with its breathtaking views of the White River Gorge, and just this morning climbed the six hundred feet of Dunn's River Falls' slippery stone steps through its cascading cold mountain water.

She'd lost track of the number of times they'd made love and where—sometimes playful, sometimes serious, always intensely satisfying. Their room, the private patio with its pool, a darkened corner of the garden behind the Jungle Room, a secluded section of the beach at twilight with the warm water lapping over them—their escapades were barely decent and still she couldn't get enough of him. She was no closer to being sated than when she started. One more day until they left. And she planned to make the most of

every minute. Tomorrow she would think about...
well, tomorrow.

Ryan crossed the room, a decidedly lecherous, lascivious light in his eyes. He slid his broad hands beneath the edge of her dress and cupped her bikini-clad
bottom.

She leaned into him, enjoying the feel of her breasts
pressing against his chest. "Do you want to go shopping in the market this afternoon?" she asked.

"We could do that." He wrapped his leg around
hers, bringing her intimately against his burgeoning
erection. "Much, much later."

"I want to look for..." She trailed off, thoroughly distracted as he stroked the underside of her leg. She
shuddered as his knuckles brushed the crotch of her bikini. The now-familiar hunger wound through her,
tightening her nipples, aching between her thighs.

His sexy laugh reverberated against her skin as he
nibbled at the base of her neck. He knew he destroyed
her reason. Just as she did his. It was a heady, fright-
ening knowledge. And she'd think about it when they
returned to the cold, gray days in Nashville.

She pulled away from his mouth, realizing a fine
sheen of perspiration coated her from the midday heat.
Unfortunately, she'd never managed to glisten dain-
tily. "I'm sweaty."

"I like it." He kissed a spot below her ear. "It turns
me on." Phoebe's laugh trailed into a sigh as his mouth
marauded her neck. His fingers bit into the back of her

thigh as he drew her closer. "*You* turn me on. So, sue me."

"I've got a much better idea. What I would like is to—" she paused, allowing him to fill in the blank before she twisted out of his arms "—race you to the pool."

Surprise afforded her a head start. She sprinted toward the patio doors.

"You'll pay for that, you little tease," Ryan yelled behind her as he gave chase.

She tore off her cover-up and slipped into the pool, the water cool against her heated skin.

"I won." She crowed as he followed her in.

"The game's not over," he taunted. "Why don't you come here? Unless you're afraid?"

Lazily, she twisted over and dove beneath the surface. Surreal. Distorted. She glided up the muscular columns of his legs, skimmed the apex of his thighs and the flat expanse of his belly, breaking the surface to stand in the circle of his arms.

Silently, of one accord, their lips met. Clinging. Tender. Exploring. The hunger was still there. But it was a slow simmer as opposed to the searing heat of the morning.

She absorbed the texture of his sun-warmed skin through her fingertips, inhaling the scent particular to him. Forever the faint aroma of chlorine on a hot day would remind her of this moment.

He led her out of the pool and up the steps to their room, leaving the French doors ajar.

"I should pay you back for earlier, but I just want to be close to you. Nothing between us." Standing in the slant of sunlight, he undressed them both, leaving the wet suits to puddle on the tile floor.

The sun backlit his broad shoulders, the narrowed line of his waist, the muscular length of his legs. Phoebe trembled with the pulsing need. Whatever tomorrow might bring, for now, for today, he was hers. She wrapped her hands around his neck and drew his mouth down, pulling him onto the bed taking his weight against her. She explored the warmth of his mouth with her tongue, memorizing his taste. She stroked the smooth, muscular line of his shoulder, imprinting the feel of him.

Ryan lifted his mouth from hers, his eyes solemn, intense, tender. He rolled onto his back, pulling her on top of him. "If I could, I would crawl inside your skin to be closer to you. Does that frighten you?" He splayed his hands against her naked back, pulling her into his chest, flattening her breasts against his hair-sprinkled plane. "It does me."

"A bit. But only because I know how you feel." His heart pounded against hers, the two rhythms blending into one.

Time assumed a new dimension. Rather than minutes and hours, time was measured in the length of a gaze between lovers, the whisper of his lips against her eyelids, the slant of sun across the back of her knees, the low murmur of his voice against her neck.

This was a symphony of lovemaking, a crescendo of flesh and spirit.

Afterward, Phoebe absently watched the shadows of a palm tree float and sway on the ceiling. That's how she felt. Weightless. Complete. Replete.

The even, measured cadence of Ryan's breathing told her he'd drifted off to sleep. She pressed her lips to the strong arm pillowing her head.

Like the lengthening shadows creeping across the ceiling, realization stole through her.

She had fallen in love with Ryan.

She had loved him for a long time. Maybe for as long as she'd known him. She had always loved him. That love had brought joy and comfort and depth to her life, and she trusted it had offered Ryan the same.

He'd been a constant. All the holidays and birthdays and school functions when her parents had promised to visit or pick her up and hadn't bothered to show or call, only to offer a lame excuse at a later date if they offered an excuse at all, Ryan had been there. And he'd done whatever it took to pull her through her parents' most recent abandonment, whether it was listen, distract, curse or amuse.

But now she had fallen in love with him. An ache blossomed in her heart. Piercing. Painful. She closed her eyes, willing away the realization. But closing her eyes didn't change anything.

She was in the worst possible place a woman could be—in love with Ryan Palmer.

STALLS LINED the narrow street. A cacophony of sounds filled the air. Some vendors hawked their wares from stalls, some from blankets spread on the ground. All haggled good-naturedly with potential buyers to the accompaniment of the ever-present rhythm of steel drums, punctuated by a chicken's occasional squawk.

Dodging a pothole, Ryan pressed closer to Phoebe's side. "Is there any chance you and Elliott will get back together once we return to Nashville?" Ryan didn't add, *once we're through.* He didn't have to. It stared both of them in the face.

Phoebe stopped in the middle of the market. Her expression plainly said she thought he'd been out in the heat too long. "Have you lost your mind?"

It was a distinct possibility. He knew it was because they were returning home tomorrow. The idea of seeing her with another man had tormented him all afternoon. And he knew it was because Elliott was the only name that came to mind. But there were plenty of other men who'd be willing to participate in her plan.

"You're sure?" He craved her reassurance.

"Why are you asking about Elliott? Are you thinking of seeing Kiki again?" Tension marked the set of her shoulders.

"Hell, no." She visibly relaxed at his emphatic assertion. "I just needed to make sure Elliott was old news. He doesn't deserve you."

"Well, thanks. I suppose."

It was odd to discuss other men with Phoebe while holding her hand, wandering through the market.

Hell, it was a strange conversation to have with any woman he was sleeping with. But then again, nothing was normal about the two of them. This ache for her that he carried around constantly wasn't normal.

The idea of another man touching her was intolerable. Even if Ryan got past that, where did this leave their friendship? When Phoebe found a new boyfriend, he might not be so tolerant of Ryan. Especially if he discovered Ryan and Phoebe had indulged in a non-platonic fling. And what happened when she moved forward with her marriage plan—which he knew she fully intended to pursue, with or without Elliott? Where did that leave Ryan?

Strolling through the market, amid street vendors and the throngs of tourists, Ryan had an epiphany. By God, he, Ryan Gerald Palmer, would marry Phoebe. She wanted a husband. He cared for her. They understood one another. The sex was great. And if he married her, that left no one to object to him.

With a whoop, Ryan caught her in his arms and spun her around. He set her on her feet, then thoroughly kissed her upturned, surprised mouth.

She blinked, laughing at him. "What was that for?"

"Just because." Now was not the time to pop the question. But he couldn't keep from grinning. She'd be so surprised. He wanted the moment to be perfect, just like his idea.

"Hmm." She wrapped her arms around his neck and kissed him, her mouth cool and sweet and faintly redolent of mint. "What are we shopping for?" She pushed her sunglasses down her nose and peered at him over them. Her brown eyes held that slightly dazed expression he'd come to recognize in the last few days. She wanted him.

He cupped his hand around the damp nape of her neck. "Spiced rum for Ted at work, and you wanted a basket and a hat."

"Oh, yeah." Although a slow, sensual smile lifted the corners of her mouth, melancholy shadowed her eyes. She pushed her glasses into place.

"You are breathtaking."

"And you are delusional." Her pleased smile and the faint flush on her cheeks belied her quip. She ran her fingertips along his jaw, sending his heartbeat thundering. "But thank you."

He caught her hand in his. It was there between them again, that quickly. The mercurial, potent head that quickened his blood. Phoebe felt it, as well. The frantic pulse at the base of her neck and the stiffened points of her nipples against the thin cotton of her dress gave her away. "Come on," he said. "Let's find you the perfect straw hat."

"Hey, mister." A street vendor hailed him in a lilting singsong. "Come take a look." She held aloft a handful of coffee bean necklaces. "Come. I sell the finest necklaces in Jamaica. Your woman, she will like this."

His woman. His Phoebe.

And after tonight there'd be no question about it.

10

"YOU'RE SURE you don't want to get in the whirlpool before dinner? It's very good for tension." Phoebe slid her top button open.

Ryan waffled, seriously tempted by her long legs, seductive smile and the promise of pulsating jets of warm water. But he wanted tonight to be absolutely perfect for them, and that meant a little planning and preparation she couldn't know about.

"I'll take a rain check. Maybe you can hold that thought until later this evening." He quickly closed the door on temptation before he lost sight of his plans and crawled in there with her.

He pulled on his pants and willed away the arousal brought on by Phoebe's proposition. He had a couple of things to take care of before tonight. Hell, it wasn't every night that a man proposed.

He let himself out of the room and checked his watch. The first thing on his agenda was to find Martin and enlist his help.

He made his way to the restaurant and sidestepped the placard deeming the restaurant closed. Martin stood folding napkins with two young men at the wait station. He looked up and spotted Ryan.

Martin crossed the room, a welcoming smile lighting his face. "How are you today? Tomorrow is your last day? I trust you have enjoyed your holiday in Jamaica."

"Jamaica's great. I love it. In fact, we'll be coming back on our honeymoon." Ryan didn't care that there was no dignity in the goofy grin on his face.

It must've been catching because Martin got a big goofy grin, as well. "Congratulations. That is most excellent. And might I offer salutations to your lucky bride-to-be, as well?"

"That's why I'm here. She doesn't know yet. Well, she probably suspects since she wants a husband. But maybe she was just trying to get my attention in the first place. And it worked." Actually, that didn't quite seem like a Phoebe-esque thing to do. But then he'd discovered other aspects of her personality he'd never considered before. And, as he'd managed to overlook for almost a lifetime, she was a woman. "I never thought when we came here..."

Martin laughed and shrugged. "It happens. Island magic. I sensed the magic between the two of you from the beginning. It was much the same way for me and my Mathilde."

It had been incredible between them. "I want something special tonight. Can you set us up with a water-side table? Maybe a little secluded?"

"I have just the spot."

"Perfect. And I'd like a bottle of Cordon Negro iced and at the table." Not the most expensive brand, but they'd certainly enjoyed it and each other in the pool. He was forgetting something. "Oh, yeah. And a ring. I can't ask her to marry me without a ring."

"Ah, yes. The ring. My cousin Angelique, she works in the gift shop here, off the lobby. She can show you many rings to choose from. There is a local artist who designs unusual jewelry. She also has choices more in keeping with tradition, such as the diamond."

"Definitely local." Perhaps when they returned to Nashville, Phoebe would want to pick out a diamond. But Jamaica was exotic braids, dazzling white sand, swimming pools at midnight and friends who became lovers. "Thanks for all your help, Martin."

"No problem. I am most honored to assist in such a memorable occasion."

Ryan grabbed his hand and pumped it. "I think it'll be a night we never forget."

"WE'RE A LITTLE EARLY for our reservations. Do you want to have a drink in the bar or a quick walk on the beach?" Ryan paused outside the restaurant, breathtakingly handsome in a lightweight summer suit. Not that it had anything to do with the suit. He'd been equally breathtaking stretched out naked on the bed earlier.

"A quick walk. The beach is practically deserted." She needed the physical activity. She was all keyed up and definitely melancholy at the prospect of leaving tomorrow. It hadn't helped her general state of mind when Ryan turned her down earlier today. It felt like the beginning of the end with them.

They veered to the path leading to the water. Phoebe stopped at the edge of the sand and slipped off her sandals. "No twisted ankles tonight."

Ryan carried his shoes and socks in one hand and slipped his other arm around her waist. Phoebe's toes curled into the sugar-fine sand, her body quickening at his touch. "I don't know. Everything turned out just fine in the end," he assured her.

They crossed the sand, Ryan's hip brushing against hers, his breath stirring the fine hairs at her temple. What woman would share his warmth and know his touch after tomorrow?

They crossed to the water's edge where the damp, packed sand was firm. Warm water swirled over their feet and lapped at their ankles. A low, thrumming urgency filled her as she recalled making love with him in a similar spot only a few evenings ago.

Arms wrapped around one another, they stopped. Phoebe absorbed the beauty and vastness of the sea stretching before them. "Isn't it beautiful? And it's amazing how constant it is. No matter what's happening in the world, this tide continues to ebb and flow."

Ryan rubbed his clean-shaven jaw against her temple. "It is beautiful. But the only constant is change. Look. No two waves are ever the same. The one that just broke over our feet is different from the one before and the one after. The tides constantly shift."

"I never thought of it that way."

They strolled along the edge of the surf. The resort buildings fronting the shoreline gave way to lush vegetation. A barely discernable order held the rampant tangle of vines and leaves in check.

Phoebe stopped. "The garden's not as controlled here by the water." Something about the place called to her. This was exactly how she felt. Barely contained. On the verge of overrunning herself. Wild. Lush. "Look. Over beyond the trees. There's a bench tucked in there."

"It's a great view of the ocean and very private. Why don't we watch the sunset?"

Phoebe paused at the edge of the sand and slipped into her strappy heels. Ryan brushed aside a branch, and they sat on the bench. The perfume of the tropical garden hung heavy around them, stirred by the ocean breeze. Faint snatches of conversation floated through the air. A fireball sun sank toward the blue-green horizon. The distant rhythm of steel drums seemed to resonate through the air, announcing their last night together.

How could she appreciate the view when she couldn't think past the press of his thigh against hers? The hot, achy hunger inside her that begged to be fed? They had so little time. Tomorrow they'd return home, and this would all be just a memory.

"Phoebe?" He breathed against her neck, his voice low and caressing, like the wash of the surf against the shore.

"Yes?"

She traced her fingernail against his cloth-covered thigh. His muscle clenched beneath her nail. That was a good sign.

"Remember the other night on the beach?"

"Yes." His thigh beneath her fingernail trembled, and his breath quickened in sync with her own. "I definitely remember." As if she'd ever forget a minute of this time with him. She wanted to make sure he never forgot, either. This was their last night. In all the years to come, she wanted him to remember making love with her as the best experience he ever had. She knew it would be, because no other woman would ever love him as deeply and fully as she did.

She slid her fingers to his inner thigh. "There's something very exciting about making love in a semipublic place. Don't you think so?"

He swelled and hardened against the back of her fingers even before he answered. "It's very...stimulating."

"If I held on to the back of the bench and you stood behind me with your jacket unbuttoned..." Her voice was low and breathless. Her knuckle traced the hard ridge of his erection. They were both on the verge of exploding.

"Stand up," he directed, his voice hoarse with excitement, his eyes bright.

Phoebe stood and walked to the back of the bench, aware of the sway of her hips, the play of her panties against her wetness. Ryan watched. The heat inside her notched up to inferno level.

She planted her feet apart, knowing her three-inch heels showed off her legs. Bracing her forearms on the back of the bench, she leaned over, her spine straight, buttocks out, and murmured in his ear, "I'm ready when you are." She laved the rim of his ear with her tongue. "Unless you've changed your mind."

"Baby, I'm so ready, I'm not sure I can walk."

"I'll be very disappointed if you can't manage to get up. I really wanted to share this view with you." She bit the lobe of his ear.

He hissed in a sharp breath. "Why don't you tell me just how disappointed you'll be," he instructed in a low, urgent tone.

"I'm all achy and hot and I'm afraid that'll just get worse if you can't join me."

Ryan stood and rounded the bench to stand behind her. Phoebe straightened, resting her hands on the back of the bench. The noise of a zipper and Ryan's harsh breathing sounded behind her. Ryan stepped closer, his stiff erection brushing her backside. Phoebe watched the glowing ball dip in the sky. Her body quivered with anticipation. Ryan eased up the back of her dress, tugging her panties to one side, wrapping one arm around her waist.

"Have you ever seen such a beautiful sunset?" he asked, thrusting into her, filling her.

She gasped. "No. It's spectacular."

His hands tightened on her hips. She leaned forward, driving him further into her. He surged again and again. She tightened around him, embracing him, telling him with her body what she could never say. Phoebe focused on the sunset until the fiery ball exploded in a dazzling array of color and disappeared into the wet depths beyond the horizon.

"That was..." Words defied her. Her legs unsteady, Phoebe tugged her dress into place.

On the beach only a few feet away, a couple strolled into view.

"Barely decent." Ryan finished her sentence as he wrapped his arms around her and nuzzled her neck, sending shivers down her spine. "And absolutely incredible."

MARTIN GREETED THEM at the door. "Right this way. We have a very special seating for you tonight. A most excellent view."

Ryan guided her with his hand on her back. A flashpoint of fire trailed through her.

This was crazy. This feverish desire for Ryan was consuming her. It was rather like having made the mistake of climbing on a ride at the fair. Caught up in the excitement, you get on and strap yourself in. The instant the ride starts, you realize you've made a mistake. But it's scary and thrilling and you don't have any choice except to stay on until the end.

Martin led them to a table overlooking the water, where a few strategically placed potted plants lent a feeling of intimacy and privacy. "And this table will please you?" Both men looked at her.

A candle flickered in the steady breeze that brushed

against her bare neck and arms. Silverware gleamed against the white linen cloth draping the table. Beyond the rail, twilight transformed the stretch of ocean to fluid turquoise.

"Yes. This is great."

Martin pulled out her chair with a flourish. "Very good, then."

Phoebe sank onto the cushion, the rattan biting into her shoulder as she shifted against the high back. Ryan sat in the chair next to her, capturing her hand in his, his fingers twining through hers. Her pulse raced. "Why don't we start with a glass of champagne? Cordon Negro?"

His gaze held hers. Memories stretched between them. Shared intimacies connected them. Phoebe traced her tongue against her lips. "That's fine."

Wasn't she capable of more speech than acquiescence? At this point, she wasn't sure. And what did she have to object to? A spectacular view? Champagne? Ryan offered everything he knew she liked.

As much as she didn't want to think about tomorrow, it kept intruding. They'd need to lay some ground rules for when they went home. She thought it best if they didn't mentioned Jamaica to each other. Let it fade like a dream. Perhaps this was the best time and place.

"Ryan..."

"Phoebe..."

"What? Go ahead." She might as well let him go first.

"We need to talk."

"Okay. What do you want to talk about?"

"I want to talk about us."

Phoebe nearly fell out of her chair. "That's my line." As a rule, men never felt compelled to talk. And Ryan was no exception. He was a man of action.

Ryan ran his hand through his hair. He only ran his hand through his hair when he was nervous. Why was he nervous?

Martin arrived with the champagne, beaming. Ryan smiled tightly at her and tugged at his tie. Definitely nervous.

As she sat through the opening and pouring of the champagne, everything fell into place. The special table. The champagne. His uneasiness. Here it was. The big dump.

Phoebe fought an insane urge to cry. It wasn't technically a dump because they'd both gone into this with their eyes open. And it was precisely what she wanted to discuss with him. It did, however, hurt a bit that Ryan felt compelled to put on the dog and pony show. For goodness' sake, this was her. Not one of the legion of other women who had come before her and who would follow behind her.

Martin retreated. Sweat beaded in a fine line across Ryan's forehead. "I didn't think this would be so difficult...."

"Oh, for pity's sake, just say it. If you don't, I will." Distress lent a sharp edge to her voice. How hard was it to say that this thing between them needed to end?

Ryan quirked an eyebrow. "I don't think we're talking about the same thing."

"We've been friends for such a long time. I think we know one another almost as well as we know ourselves. I assure you, there's no need to keep hedging around. We're on the same track."

He looked surprised and relieved. Good grief, was he always so uptight about ending a physical relationship?

"Good. So, when do you want to get married?"

"There, that wasn't so hard—" Her mouth stopped moving as she scrambled to assimilate what he'd said instead of what she'd anticipated. She almost laughed. She could've sworn he'd said *married*. Nah. No way had she heard what—well, what she thought she'd heard. "What did you say?"

"Let's get married."

Nothing wrong with her ears. Her life was falling apart but her hearing was fine.

"Married?" Her voice rose several octaves, squawking in the night air. At nearby tables, several diners looked over at them. Phoebe lowered her voice, "Did you say married?"

"Married. Tie the knot. Step up to the plate. Married."

Two weeks ago, he could barely utter the word. Now he was tossing it around the table with abandon. Her stomach roiled in protest. She couldn't have heard him right.

"So, who do you want to marry?"

He laughingly admonished her. "Stop fooling around, Phoebe." His laughter died out, and he peered into her face. "You're not fooling around, are you? You. I want to marry you."

"You and me? To each other?" She wasn't slow on the uptake. It simply didn't make sense. She had obviously misunderstood him somewhere along the line.

"You and me. Us." His expression bordered on smug.

Phoebe contained her rising hysteria. Ryan Palmer had just proposed. My God. A vacation fling was one thing. Long-term commitment was another. And this, coming from Ryan, the king of short-term commitments. "Why?" She barely managed to utter the word. She picked up her glass and gulped the champagne.

"Hey. We're supposed to toast our engagement with that as soon as you say yes." Uncertainty replaced his smugness.

"Sorry. I need a drink now." She drained the glass.

"I thought you'd be excited."

Try appalled. "I'm practically speechless."

"I noticed," he said with more than a note of asperity.

"Why would we want to marry each other?" She tried to keep her tone light, neutral, conversational, as if they were discussing the weather rather than matrimony. But just saying the words made her queasy.

His usual easygoing demeanor gave way to a frown of annoyance. "But you said you wanted to get married."

"Yes. And do you remember the other part? Start a family?"

He waved a hand in the air. "Okay. In a couple of years we'll talk about a kid."

She struggled to make some sense of the incomprehensible—Ryan's proposal and willingness to start a family.

"Why?"

"Damn, Phoebe. Is that all you can say? *Why?* Because you want one."

"You're not making any sense. We can't get married and have kids just because I want to. We're friends." She couldn't allow herself to give in to the temptation of imagining a life with him.

She poured another glass of champagne.

"Now you're the one that's not making any sense. Why can't friends get married?"

God, they were talking in circles, and if they didn't cut to the chase, she was going to make a spectacle of them both by screaming. "Forget about that. I want to know why *we* should get married."

"Think about it. We like one another. We get along great." He lowered his voice and leaned closer. "And the sex is phenomenal."

Even in the middle of a breakdown, he reduced her to hot candle wax with a single touch and a searing glance. Phoebe reveled in the phenomenal sex ranking for just a second before she discounted his reasoning. "You can't marry someone because the sex is good."

"Great."

"Okay. Great. It's still no reason to get married."

"What's going to happen to us, Phoebe? Stop and think about it. Your next boyfriend may not be so tolerant of our friendship, especially after this week. I sure as hell wouldn't. Have you given up your marriage plan?"

"So, you want to get married because my next boyfriend or possibly my husband will object to our friendship because we've been lovers?"

"Exactly. You're very important to me, Phoebes."
Nowhere along the way had he mentioned love or being in love. Up until this point, she'd been somewhat confounded. Now she was simply angry. Of all the high-handed, arrogant maneuvers... "Ah, I see. Protecting your interests?"

"Not exactly. That makes it sound..."

"Selfish? Absurd?"

"I wouldn't put it quite like that."

"Oh, really? How would you put it?"

"Sensible. Reasonable. You're normally so rational—"

"Are you implying that I'm behaving irrationally?"
Perhaps a tad tipsy after two glasses of champagne on an empty stomach but certainly not irrational. Nowhere near as irrational as the idea of the two of them marrying one another.

"Don't put words in my mouth."

"I'm not. You're doing a fine job all on your own."

"Dammit, Phoebe, it's a good plan. We understand

one another, we care about one another. Why wouldn't it work?"

She'd never been very good in debate club. She detested presenting arguments. Things that made sense to her often lost their impact in the translation. But this was important. She'd try to make him understand.

"Do you have any idea how much you mean to me? Do you know how important our friendship is?" Tears pricked at the back of her eyelids, sprung from the desperation, confusion and frustration welling inside her. She bit her lip. Hard. She would not cry.

"All the more reason to get married."

"All the more reason not to. We'll weather this...this...this fling. We can still come back from this, but a bad marriage would destroy us, and you're too important to me for that." Her bond with Ryan was the only one she'd allowed herself since her parents had abandoned her. She'd often thought how much easier it would've been had they died rather than just dropping her off. Then all hope would've died with them. The thought of losing Ryan was unbearable.

"Why are you assuming we'd have a bad marriage?"

"Marriage is a long-term commitment. You yourself have said how fond you are of changing channels. I won't sit around and wait for you to switch to another channel." Or sit around hoping he'd come back if he did. She didn't exactly inspire those near and dear to stick around.

"That's not fair. This is different. How long have we

been friends? Don't you consider that a long-term commitment?"

"Friendship is one thing. Marriage is another." She didn't want to hurt him, but they'd always been honest with one another and the stakes were high. Even though they sat in the open air, she felt trapped. She couldn't bear to sit at the table another second. "You're the best friend I've ever had. The best friend I'll ever have." She scraped her chair back and stood. "But you're the last man I'd choose for a husband."

11

RYAN FOUND HER easily enough, standing alone, silhouetted by the moonlight against the shoreline. He squared his shoulders. She'd sliced through his pride, but he refused to leave things this way between them.

And he really didn't give a damn that she'd left him standing there like a fool. Well, maybe he gave a little bit of a damn, but she couldn't dissuade him that easily.

Sand crept into his shoes as he crossed to where Phoebe stood, her arms wrapped around her middle, looking out over the dark expanse of water. He stood behind her, not touching her. She knew he was there. He felt her acknowledgment of him in the space between them.

She spoke without turning. "I know you're angry. And hurt. I didn't want either one." Emotion thickened her voice. "I didn't expect you to walk down here."

He cupped his hands around her shoulders, her bare skin smooth as silk beneath his palms, and pulled her against him. She held herself stiffly. As if she wouldn't allow herself to lean on him. He stood for a moment, the length of her lightly against him, her braids against his face, absorbing her scent and the emotions that rolled off of her like waves crashing in a storm-tossed sea.

"How could I leave things between us that way? I can't. You mean too much to me."

"God, how did things get to be such a mess between us?" Her voice cracked on the last word, wrenching something deep inside him. The last thing he'd ever wanted was to hurt her.

"It's just different. It's a change. You know you don't handle change well. And this is a biggie. But I'll help you. We'll help each other. Because that's what we do."

He turned her to face him and wrapped his arms around her, drawing her close. He took heart that she allowed him to hold her. Her face was wet against his neck when she leaned into him. He stroked her head with one hand. "Shh. It's okay. It's all going to be fine."

"How?" Her low keen rent the night. "How will things ever be the way they were between us again?"

"They won't." Things would never be the way they were before they'd made love. "They'll be better. Have you thought of it that way?"

He could practically feel the fear surrounding her, prickling her skin beneath his fingertips. "No." Desperation and denial resounded in her voice. "If we just try, we can get back to where we were."

A light went off in his head. She wasn't moving forward when they'd slept together, embracing a new phase of their relationship. She'd been scrambling like hell to get back to where they'd come from. She wasn't going out on a limb, she was running in a circle.

"Listen to yourself. You want to go back and you can't, Phoebe. Life is all about moving forward. Change is a good thing."

"That's the problem. That's why it would never work between us. You can't live your life without change. You're addicted to it. What happens when you get tired of me as a wife? When the phenomenal sex isn't so phenomenal anymore? Do you think we can go back to being friends after that? I'm not one of your women that will hang around in the harem afterward."

Ryan let the harem comment pass. As a rule, his breakups weren't nasty, but he sure as hell didn't have a harem. "So, how do you see it happening now? I don't understand the difference."

"The difference is in the level of commitment and trust. It takes a little more to be a husband than a friend."

He dropped his arms to his side. "So, you don't trust me emotionally." That hurt. "I've got what it takes to be your friend. And as a lover, you seem fairly satisfied. But I'm not marriage material. Thanks, Phoebe."

"Look at your track record with women."

"There were a lot of fish in the sea, and I enjoyed fishing." That sounded lame even to him. Hell, there'd been a lot of women before her, and unfortunately, she knew about each and every one of them.

"But now you're ready to put away your rod? I don't think so. Those fish are still out there."

"I've never asked another woman to marry me. I've never felt this way about anyone else. And I never will."

A cloud covered the moon, pitching the beach in darkness.

"It's a temporary aberration."

"You're the one that I want. The only one." He could be as damned stubborn as Phoebe.

"Perhaps you should listen to yourself. I may be the one with the reputation for competitiveness, but you're the consummate competitor. Don't destroy our friendship just because you won't allow me to be the one who got away."

Ryan wasn't the best salesman in the southeast for nothing. He knew when to back off. He'd let his pitch rest. "Okay. We'll let it drop for now."

But Phoebe better be prepared. Because he wasn't about to lose the best thing that ever happened to him.

TWELVE HOURS.

Twelve hours until they climbed on a shuttle bus and headed for the airport. Twelve hours until this crazy ride ended and she climbed off.

Tomorrow was another day. Tomorrow she'd think about Ryan's proposal. Tomorrow she'd lose her braids. Tomorrow she'd figure out their friendship.

But for tonight she wanted her lover.

"I know we'd planned to go to the beach party and

then the Jungle Room tonight. But I just want to go back to the room."

Quite frankly, she felt far too emotionally raw for either one.

He skimmed his hand along the length of her side and rested it on her hip. "I'm not interested in the beach party or the Jungle Room. I just want to be with you."

Her breath caught in her throat. "That's what I was thinking, as well." They did still agree on *some* things.

Silently they made their way to the room, wrapped in the distant sounds of revelry and the dark of the night.

The door closed behind them, wrapping them in the intimacy of their room. The imminent return to Nashville, Ryan's proposal and Phoebe's refusal all flavored the atmosphere with a hint of desperation and borrowed time.

Ryan dropped to the chaise. He caught Phoebe's hand and pulled her onto his lap.

"Phoebe..." He sounded as urgent as she felt. He cupped the back of her neck, drawing her mouth to his.

She wrapped her arms around his neck and lost herself in his kiss. In the subtle play of his lips slanting against hers. By tacit agreement, it was a leisurely exploration. She gave herself over to his long, slow, drugging kisses.

Phoebe rested her head against his shoulder. Tonight she would say all the things she couldn't tomorrow. "You're a great kisser."

"You are eminently kissable." He captured her mouth again.

Phoebe rimmed the inside of his mouth with her tongue. Deep, satisfying strokes. His heart pounded beneath her shoulder.

"Phoebes..."

"Hmm?" She'd be content to sit here making out with him all night. Well, maybe not making out all night. But a large portion. He kissed like nobody's business. After tomorrow, it wouldn't be her business.

"Is it like this for you with other men?" His eyes were intent.

"You can't ask me that."

"Why the hell not? We seem to be making up our own rules as we go along. You had me rate our sex together."

"Okay. No. It's not." She'd always considered her sex drive healthy, but making love with Ryan bordered on an obsession. She traced the line of his brow with her finger. "It's never been this way before with anyone else. Only you."

"It's never been this way for me with anyone else, either."

"I don't want to talk." She scattered short, tiny kisses along his cheek, the line of his jaw. "We can talk later."

Later there'd be no sweet, slow kisses on his lap. And she still had enough brain cells left to realize that sexy, seductive Ryan was working her. That was fine. She wanted to be worked.

He slipped her dress off one shoulder. "If you don't want to talk, what do you want to do?"

She slid off his lap and stood before him. Reaching behind her, she tugged down the zipper, thankful the back was low cut and she didn't have to go through any funky contortions to get to the thing. She slid the dress off first one shoulder, then the other, letting it hang for a few tantalizing seconds on her breasts.

Ryan swallowed hard, a feral expression on his face. She let the front drop and shimmied, sending it past her hips to pool around her feet. Standing in front of him, wearing only high-heeled sandals, a thong and a Wonderbra, she didn't think he could possibly be confused as to what she wanted to do.

However, just to dispel any lingering doubts, she murmured, "We have a few of those chocolate-covered doughnuts left, and the diet starts tomorrow."

RYAN STUFFED his last pair of shorts into his suitcase and zipped it. "Ready?"

Phoebe, propped against the doorjamb, staring at the pool, turned. "Sure. I'm ready."

They'd made love off and on all night and then again this morning in the shower. Far from being worn out, they'd been desperate for one another this morning.

The fleeting thought had occurred to him that if they screwed one another to death, they wouldn't have to worry about what happened afterward. However, that hadn't happened. By the time she'd finished packing, Phoebe had surrounded herself with a wall built of distance, mortared by friendly cheer that had him gritting his teeth.

"So, why don't we bring our leftover doughnuts with us? It seems a shame to just leave them here." Hell, it didn't hurt to ask.

She shook her head. "I don't think so." She offered the first real smile he'd seen in the last hour. "But that was a nice try."

Ryan shrugged, hoping he appeared more nonchalant than he felt. "Can't blame a guy for trying."

Her hand was on the doorknob when he did some quick thinking. "Whoa." She turned to face him. "I just wanted to remind you that Kiki and Elliott will be on the shuttle, and we all have seats together on the flight. They'll be watching us."

He'd like to say that he didn't give a crap what Kiki and Elliott thought, but that wasn't strictly true. He didn't want Elliott getting the idea that Phoebe was available. She wasn't. She might consider herself available, but he knew better. After all, it was just a matter of convincing her. And he damn well didn't need Elliott nosing around while Ryan was busy doing that convincing. Plus it gave him a reason to touch her and work on wearing down her defenses.

"I'd forgotten all about them."

It was a small detail, but it offered more than a generous measure of hope when ultracompetitive Phoebe admitted she'd forgotten about the competition.

"Well, let's make this easy on both of us. Let's bring our doughnuts as far as Nashville."

"They get left at the airport."

"At the airport. Gone. Deal?"

"Deal."

"Then we need to take care of this." He braced his hands on the door on either side of her, effectively trapping her. He leaned in, inhaling her scent, breathing in the moist heat of her breath, heartened by the flare of passion in her eyes. "Can't have you looking neglected."

"PHOEBE." Ryan shook her. "Baby, wake up. We're circling to land."

Leaning against his chest, her head pillowed on his shoulder, Phoebe reluctantly shook off the last vestiges of sleep.

"Uh-huh." She didn't open her eyes immediately. She took a few last seconds to soak up his warmth, the scent of him overlaying his aftershave, the rhythm of his hearbeat, the texture of his skin.

She opened her eyes and sat up. Ryan moved his arm from around her to reach over and click first her seat belt in place and then his. "You slept most of the way. Do you feel better?"

"I didn't realize how tired I was." She had fallen into an exhausted sleep once the plane took off.

"It was all that physical activity. Besides, you didn't get any sleep last night. And not a whole lot the night before." Ryan nibbled along her jaw.

Phoebe caught a movement in the row behind them. Elliott. Eavesdropping.

She nipped at Ryan's mouth with a playful kiss. "Sorry I kept you up all night."

"Mmm. It was a pleasure."

"Yes, it was."

She was pathetic. There was no other word for it. Here she and Ryan were, putting on a show for the benefit of Kiki and Elliott behind them, and she was enjoying her last few desperate moments of intimacy with Ryan. A few suggestive phrases, a tender touch and she wanted him again.

Without considering the wisdom of her actions, her eyes dropped to his crotch. Oh. He was in the same boat she was.

"Phoebe." Ryan's voice was as strained as the front of his jeans.

Caught up in Ryan, Phoebe was quite surprised when the plane touched down and braked along the runway. While the flight attendant ran through her spiel on the intercom, Ryan whispered in Phoebe's ear. "Baby, if you don't stop looking at me, or more specifically *it*, like that, I'm not going to be able to walk off the plane without embarrassing both of us."

"Oh."

They taxied to a stop at the gate. There was the awkward stretch of waiting in front of Kiki and Elliott for overhead bin luggage to be removed and the passengers ahead of them to disembark.

"Well, I have to say this was a different week than I imagined," Kiki offered.

And just what did you say to the woman who'd

hopped into bed with your boyfriend, expecting you to join them, the woman who'd essentially started the whole ball rolling? Phoebe smiled. "I never dreamed it could be so good."

Elliott, standing behind Kiki, flushed. Ryan turned and draped his arm possessively over Phoebe's shoulder, "It was the best week of my life."

Kiki smiled at Ryan. "Call me sometime."

Jealousy, white-hot and cutting, surged through Phoebe. For one insane, irrational moment her hand flexed, intent on slapping the leer right off Kiki's gorgeous face.

"I don't think so." Ryan's lack of interest, sanity and a moving stream of passengers saved her from herself.

Phoebe walked down the plane's narrow aisle. *That* was why she and Ryan could never make it as a couple. He was like a pot of honey to a horde of flies. Women liked him. Wanted him. So he wasn't interested in Kiki now. What about later? What about the next woman who hit on him? What about the fifth or sixth woman? It wasn't Ryan's fault that women liked him. And he liked them in return—for a while. Since his first girlfriend in high school, he'd never dated one woman more than a few weeks. He'd set a record a few years ago with a redhead named Judy. They'd dated a month.

She stepped into the chilly tunnel leading to the terminal.

Ryan was right behind her. "Phoebes, wait. I told her I didn't want to call."

Phoebe slowed down. It really wasn't his fault. It was just the way things were. So she did the next best thing to slapping Kiki. She slipped her arm around Ryan's waist as if she had every right to.

They stepped into the terminal, and she pulled him to one side and wrapped her arms around him, kissing him square on the mouth. Let Kiki take that home with her. His mouth was warm and, after his initial start of surprise, he was a willing participant.

Phoebe lost track of time, place, and wasn't too certain of her name. Kissing Ryan tended to affect her that way.

12

PHOEBE UNLOCKED the door to her condo, and Bridgette ran in ahead of her, settling in her favorite spot in front of the couch, obviously glad to be home. Phoebe followed, already missing Jamaica, or more specifically, Ryan.

Nashville was cold and rainy. Even her condo, which always seemed so comfortable, was cool and damp. She dragged her suitcase to the middle of the room and kicked off her shoes. She hit the flashing red light on her answering machine and listened to her messages while she set up a fire to dispel the chill.

"Hi, honey. It's me, Aunt Caroline. You know I hate talking to this thing but I just wanted to say I hope you had a good time. I want to hear all about your trip sometime next week. Why don't you plan on coming by for dinner on Tuesday night? And bring Bridgette with you. We enjoyed her company."

Aunt Caroline and Uncle Frank had been out for their regular Sunday afternoon hike when she'd dropped by to pick up Bridgette. Phoebe felt guilty over how relieved she'd been that they weren't home. She'd have to practice a travelogue before she went over Tuesday night.

With the fire off to a crackling start, she plopped onto the sofa. She rubbed her toes along Bridgette's back. The dog sighed happily.

Message number two was a mortgage telemarketer promising to save her money if she refinanced with his company. She skipped ahead to number three, a reminder from her dentist's office to schedule a cleaning.

Message four. "Phoebes, I wanted to make sure you got in okay. Call me when you get home." Ryan.

The sound of his voice, rich, smooth, with a hint of a Southern drawl, washed over her like the warm waters of the Caribbean. It wasn't a message from her friend. It was a message from her lover. Just the sound of his voice evoked a landslide of memories and emotions that besieged her good sense and left her breathless.

In the midst of gathering her remaining wits, the phone rang again. Aunt Caroline? Ryan? She almost wished for a telemarketer, which was probably a first in consumer history and just went to show the depth of her deprivation.

"Hello."

"Phoebes." Ryan. Her stomach flip-flopped. "Did you just get in?"

"I was listening to my messages."

"Listen, baby, about—"

"Ryan." She interrupted him, her pulse pounding like those steel drums they'd left behind in Jamaica. "You can't call me that."

"What?"

"Baby."

"Oh?"

"Yeah. It's too...it's not..." How about provocative? Sexy? It brought to mind a steamy shower against a marble wall, champagne in a private pool, a Caribbean sunset she'd never forget. "How about you just don't call me that. Let's stick with Phoebe. Okay?"

"I'll try."

"Try hard." She closed her eyes. Poor adjective choice. Freud would have a field day with that.

"For you, I'll try very hard."

Evil lurked in his soul. Well, evil wasn't exactly the word for it. But she recognized the interest in his voice. He was in the same sorry state she was. His eyes would be narrowed, his face taking on that hard look. He was trying to seduce her over the phone.

"I personally think you're at your best when it's hard." She should've never said that, but good grief, she missed him. It had been hours since they showered this morning.

"Things are very hard for me right now."

"I think we've digressed."

"I think there's another word for it." His sexy, teasing note curled through her.

"Behave."

"You started it."

"No, I...well, I suppose I did. Sorry. It won't happen again."

"I hate to hear that."

"Stop. That's exactly the kind of thing we have to watch."

"Okay, baby—"

"No baby. Remember?"

"Oh, yeah. So, where were we before we wandered down the path of telephone perdition?"

"You were just calling to make sure I got home."

"Oh, yeah." Silence stretched across the line. "I miss you, Phoebes." His voice was quiet and low.

It had been all of what? two hours? She missed him desperately also. "It's Sunday afternoon. Do you want to come over?" There was nothing suggestive at all in her invitation. He usually came over on Sunday afternoons for an early dinner. And what difference would one more day make?

"I could pick up a pizza on the way over."

"Double cheese with anchovies?"

"I thought you'd want light cheese with roasted veggies."

"I'm starting my diet tomorrow."

"Oh." A wealth of meaning came through in that one word. "I'll pick up a box of chocolate-covered doughnuts, as well."

"That's always a good way to start a diet."

"I'll be there within an hour." He hung up before she could answer.

This was the downside to diving into the murky waters of sleeping with your best friend. Who the hell were you supposed to talk to about it? And she desperately needed to talk.

She'd always been very private. And while she had lots of acquaintances she could call up for dinner or a movie, Ryan was her true friend. Bridgette was a decent listener, but not very forthcoming with advice. It was fairly difficult to bounce ideas off a dog.

She supposed she'd have to start talking to herself. She caught a glimpse of her braided reflection in the window. Perhaps that was part of her problem. She was still in the Jamaican mind-set.

"The first step is to lose the braids. Who knows, maybe all the magic was tied up in Jamaica. Maybe things will be just like they were before."

Bridgette lifted her head, then lowered it again, closing her eyes.

Phoebe didn't think so, either.

RYAN BALANCED pizza, doughnuts and a six-pack of beer and knocked on Phoebe's door.

It wasn't as if he was desperate to see her or anything. He'd called, and she'd invited him over. Same as every Sunday.

Locks turned on the other side, and she threw the door open. "Hi."

"Pizza. Doughnuts. Beer." He hefted the cartons. "The essentials." God, he sounded pathetic.

She stepped aside. "Come on in."

The door closed behind him and he stood stock-still on the foyer's parquet floor, drinking in the sight of her. She wore faded plaid boxers, an old college T-shirt, no bra—he could see the soft round mounds of her breasts and the outline of her nipples—and her unbraided hair hung in wet rat tails around her head.

He'd bet she wasn't wearing any panties underneath those boxers, either. She looked delectable.

While he was looking, her nipples hardened and thrust against the front of her T-shirt. Phoebe was doing terrible things to his blood pressure. She was like his own all-natural version of Viagra.

"Just put it on the coffee table." She gestured toward the other room.

"I see you got rid of your braids."

"I told you I would. That was Jamaica. This is Nashville."

Yeah. He got the message loud and clear. He put the boxes on the table and bent to scratch Bridgette behind the ears. "How are you, girl? How'd you get along with all those cats?" Bridgette licked his hand.

"Want to watch the game?" he called.

"Sure."

He turned on the TV while she rounded up paper plates. "Beer?" she called from the kitchen.

"Sounds good.

She came in balancing plates, napkins, silverware and two beers. Ryan grabbed for the beers as they began to topple. He caught them in the nick of time, his finger skimming her nipple.

"Sorry." His heart thundered like that of an adolescent boy with a girlie magazine.

Phoebe sucked in her breath. "Don't worry about it." She dumped the stuff on the table, the silverware clattering on the glass top. "So, what channel is the game on?"

"Try five." Ryan sat on one end of the couch and lifted the lid on the pizza. He wasn't particularly hungry, but it gave him something to do other than stare at Phoebe and the jiggle of her breasts against the stretch of her T-shirt.

He and Phoebe went through the motions. They bet on the outcome of the game, ate a slice of pizza, each drank a beer and cheered on their respective teams.

No tropical breeze blew in over a sparkling sea. Her ceiling fan didn't work. The motor had burned out in the fall, and she hadn't gotten around to replacing it.

No steel drums pulsated in the background. Twelve men beat the hell out of one another on a field of ice while fans screamed from the stands.

She wasn't wearing high-heeled sandals, a thong and a Wonderbra. Her clothes were worn and old, and her feet were bare.

Her hair wasn't in sexy cornrows. It had dried pretty much the way it was after she ran a towel through it.

They weren't in exotic Jamaica. They were in cold, gray Nashville.

It should've been just like old times.

It wasn't.

Ryan wanted her so badly he could hardly see straight.

Tension. Awareness. Want. Need. Stretched between them.

"Want a doughnut?" He hadn't meant for it to come out so abruptly.

"I thought you'd never ask."

Neither of them glanced at the box on the table. Ryan reached her in mid launch. He buried his hands in the damp silk of her hair, his mouth devouring hers. She molded her hands to the back of his head, forcing him closer.

Both panting, chests heaving, they came up for air. He rested his forehead against hers. "Oh, baby. I missed you."

Whatever it was between them may have started in Jamaica, but it definitely hadn't ended there.

PHOEBE ENTERED Birelli's, just as she'd done for the last seven years, for lunch with Ryan on Thursday at twelve-thirty. Over the course of those seven years, she'd arrived elated with good news, depressed with bad news, frustrated with her job, current boyfriend or parents. But until today, she'd never arrived nervous.

She tried to quiet the butterflies in her stomach. This nervousness was silly. Almost as silly as her decision to forgo panty hose this morning in favor of stockings and a flirty garter belt.

Ryan was at the same table they sat at each week. He looked up from a report as she dropped onto the stool opposite him. "Hey. You made it."

"Yeah. So did you." Feeling ridiculously adolescent, she devoured him with her eyes. As if she hadn't seen him a mere four days ago, she noted the sexy quirk of his lips, the hug of his button-down across his broad shoulders, the gleam in his pale green eyes.

Naomi sauntered over with two glasses of tea. "Here

you are. The stromboli'll be out in a minute. How was—" She stopped abruptly, glancing back and forth between Ryan and Phoebe. "Lord have mercy. Ya'll did it, didn't you?" She didn't wait for confirmation. Holding her tray in one hand, she pumped the other hand in the air. "Yes! I've won a ton of money. We've had this pool going on ya'll for the last couple of years. I knew it was just a matter of time. Wait until I tell George." Naomi hurried off in the direction of the kitchen and George, the cook.

Great. Phoebe'd obviously picked up a banner proclaiming she'd slept with Ryan Palmer. She smiled tightly at the other customers staring at them. A slow burn heated her face.

Ryan shrugged. "Don't worry about it, baby." He held up a hand. "Sorry, I forgot."

Naomi bore down on them again. "Here you are. One stromboli. One salad with bread sticks. And it's on the house today."

"Naomi, we can't—"

"Trust me, I can afford it today. Thanks to you two." She cut off Phoebe's protest. "Ya'll enjoy."

Ryan sliced off a neat quarter of the stromboli. Instead of transferring it to another plate, he picked it up, stringing the melted cheese along the way. "Here."

She leaned forward and bit into the crusty bread filled with gooey cheese, her teeth scraping against his finger. The laughter in his eyes faded, replaced by a hunger that had nothing to do with stromboli.

They didn't exchange tales about work or co-workers. Instead, lunch passed in a haze of desperation and desire. Phoebe sat across from Ryan, aware of each brush of his trousered leg against her stockinged legs, the scent of his aftershave, the cadence of his voice, the tension enveloping them in a cocoon of intimacy.

"Baklava?"

Phoebe made a pretense of checking her watch. "None for me. I really need to get back to the office."

"We'll skip it today. Thanks, Naomi."

"No, thank you. Both of you." She dropped a wink at them. "Enjoy the rest of your lunch."

They stood. Ryan followed Phoebe, his hand resting against the small of her back, his fingers burning through her suit fabric.

They both paused on the sidewalk. Ryan's hand slid to her hip in a possessive gesture.

"Where'd you park?" Ryan asked, his mouth close enough to her ear to send shivers down her spine.

"Two blocks over, on Thurston. It was crowded."

"I'm right across the street in the parking garage. Why don't I give you a ride?"

They crossed the street and waited silently for the garage elevator. Phoebe took great care not to touch him, not quite sure that she wouldn't come unhinged. How could it possibly be only four days since she'd touched him, tasted him, breathed his scent and marked him as her own? It felt like a lifetime.

The doors opened, and a businessman stepped off, checking his watch. Ryan pushed the fourth-floor button. The doors had barely closed before they fell on one another.

His mouth was hot and hard against hers, just like his body pressing her against the elevator wall. Phoebe ground against him. He dove beneath her skirt with his hands and clutched her.

The elevator bell rang, announcing their stop on the fourth floor. They tore themselves apart. Panting. Frantic.

"Where's the car?"

"Back in that corner. On the other side of that big truck."

"Hurry."

Phoebe practically dragged him along the row of parked cars.

"Passenger side," Ryan instructed as he rounded the car and unlocked the door. He opened it, fell into the seat, then tugged Phoebe onto his lap. He slammed the door closed, killed the dome light and threw the seat into the recline position.

Phoebe hiked her skirt up and straddled him, leaving her thighs bare and open to his view.

If she hadn't been wet before, the look of absolute lust and appreciation darkening his eyes would've done the trick. The garter belt and stockings were a big hit. "Oh, baby," he groaned, one hand on his zipper, the other on the back of her thigh.

Phoebe held his head between her hands and kissed him hard. Her teeth ground against his. Her tongue plunged into his mouth. Ryan fisted his hand in her panties and dragged them to one side. With his other hand, Ryan positioned her over his erection. In one downward surge, she filled herself with him. Hot, sweet emotion raged through her, escaping in a keening moan that he absorbed. Within seconds they both found the release in each other they so craved.

Spent, Phoebe collapsed on top of him, unsure where the pounding of his heart began and hers ended.

God, she loved him.

PHOEBE CLIMBED out of her car, a little perplexed and a lot frustrated. Why Ryan wanted to meet at a municipal park on a blustery day on the tail end of winter was beyond her. She was all achy, and there wasn't going to be much opportunity to assuage that ache here. Of course, making love with Ryan never assuaged it. But it did keep it manageable. She wouldn't even get that today. Unless they found a nice remote spot for the car. Her blood pumped a little faster at the thought.

Ryan waited for her at a bench overlooking a duck pond, his jacket collar turned up against the cold. Only a handful of hardy ducks braved the water this early. The wind whistled eerily through bare limbs with a chill that chased down her spine. Two joggers in winter gear ran along the winding path. A couple of mothers and their bundled children were at the playground.

"Hi." Phoebe shivered into her coat. "It's brisk out here. Why don't we go sit in my car?"

Ryan stood to greet her but didn't touch her. "No. It's too easy to get distracted. That's why I wanted to meet here today. There's not much opportunity for distraction," he said without his customary grin.

Sinking to the bench, she didn't offer a smile, either. She had a very bad feeling about this. Ryan sat beside her.

"Phoebe, we've got to talk," he stated baldly.

Oh, boy. She was growing to really hate it when he said that.

He ran his hand through his hair. Phoebe hoped the primal scream rising inside her wouldn't find its way out. She steeled herself.

"This isn't working."

Her stomach clenched in protest even though she'd known this day was coming. She'd known before the first kiss. She'd known he would leave her. Ryan was a short-term kind of guy, and she seemed to have that effect on people. She checked the date on her watch with a tight smile. "Fourteen days. A bit shorter than I thought we'd last. I was hoping we could go for a personal record with you, a little over a month. But I guess it's not to be."

Jesus. She sounded hateful and bitchy and more than a little spiteful. But it beat the hell out of sobbing like a baby and begging him not to end things, which was what she felt like doing. She absolutely would not beg.

"Dammit. Would you listen?"

"You have my undivided attention." Or what was left that hadn't already died inside.

"We can't keep going on like this. We can't just keep having sex."

"But that's all..."

"That's what I mean. We get together all the time, although calling our encounters dates is a stretch." A hint of bitterness curled his lips. "Sometimes for lunch, occasionally for a movie, always for sex. The sex is great, but that's all we have anymore. The closer we get physically, the further away you slip emotionally. Can't you feel it? This is destroying us."

"Well, that's a unique breakup approach." She felt a searing pain and a horrible hollowness. She knew he was right.

"Every time I try to bring up the dreaded *m* word, we wind up distracted. We're not distracted now. Marry me."

Anything that hurt this bad now would be unbearable in six months or a year down the road.

"No."

Ryan brushed her cheek with his gloved thumb. She could swear she felt his heat against her skin through the black leather. "Phoebe, I've waited all my life for you. All the other women were a crazy attempt to run from what was staring me in the face. You. Don't you see? They were all the exact opposite of you. Of course none of them lasted. It wasn't meant to be. I suppose I'm a little slow, but I've finally figured it out. You're all I've ever wanted. You're all I'll ever want. I love you. I'm so in love with you, I ache."

She had firsthand knowledge of aching. However,

emotional cauterization reduced her to monosyllables. "No."

"Phoebe, you love me." He took her hands in his, the desperate tenor of his voice at odds with the children's ringing laughter on the playground. "And I'm pretty damn sure you're in love with me."

Her hands lay limp in his, and she looked at him. She hoped he finished soon. She felt she at least owed him that, but she couldn't stand much more of this.

"Baby, there's always been this connection between us. Since the first time I found you crying in the woods behind my house. Remember Jamaica? Remember looking out at the Caribbean? Our relationship is like the ocean. The tides change. Sometimes it's calm. Sometimes it's stormy. But it's always there."

She'd been waiting for this to come. Waiting for the other shoe to drop. Just as she'd known it was coming with Elliott. She'd known from the beginning he'd walk away from her. "That's a lovely analogy. I wish I could buy into it—and you're a very persuasive salesman—but I can't."

"Phoebes, don't do this to us."

"I'm not the one doing this. You're the one laying down ultimatums. Didn't you say marriage or nothing?" He wanted more than she could give. He wanted her to step out farther on that limb than she could go.

"I've tried it your way, Phoebes. It's not enough. I want to wake up and feel your warmth next to me every morning. I want to grow old with you."

"I just don't think we can have those things."

"You know what I think?" She was certain she was about to find out. She was equally certain she wasn't going to appreciate his opinion. "I think you're so damn scared you can't see straight. When we were friends, that was nice and safe, wasn't it, Phoebes? You can still maintain a comfortable distance with your friends. The men you've dated? No emotional depth there. All nice, safe, distant choices. It didn't really hurt when Elliott defected, did it, Phoebes?"

Anger displaced her debilitating numbness. "How about you? With your revolving-door relationships? Like there's some emotional investment there? Don't make me laugh," Phoebe said.

He nodded, his face hard. "At least I can admit it. You hold everyone at arm's length. Your aunt Caroline and uncle Frank. Me. Your co-workers. Not too long before we left for Jamaica, you told me I was emotionally retarded and you were the enabler. Hell, maybe I am emotionally retarded. But you need to step back and take a good, hard look at yourself. Because you were looking in the mirror, not at me. You know why I'm the last man you'd want to marry? Hide behind my track record if it makes you feel good. But the truth is, you don't want to marry me because you'd feel too damn much, Phoebe."

She held her backbone ramrod stiff, otherwise it'd crumple and she'd die in a pile right before him. "Well, I hope you feel better. I don't."

"It's not about feeling better. It's about saving us."

"So, that's your offer? Marriage or nothing?"

13

RYAN SAT at the table in Birelli's, ostensibly reviewing last month's production report. It had been two days since they'd met in the park. He hadn't called. She hadn't called. No take-out Chinese. No hockey games. No sex. No Phoebe.

He'd be lying like a big dog if he said he didn't miss the sex. Just the thought of a parking garage gave him a hard-on. But what he really missed was Phoebe. It was as if he'd amputated an essential body part.

Naomi stopped by the table and checked her watch, "She's late. Where is she? She's never late."

"I don't know if she's coming." Ryan spoke the words he'd avoided facing.

Naomi snatched Phoebe's glass of ice tea, swiping the puddle beneath it. Most of the ice had melted. "She'll be here." She thunked the glass onto the table. "There she is now. I told you'd she'd come," Naomi said.

Ryan spotted Phoebe on the sidewalk through the glass windows of the restaurant. He felt nauseous with relief. He could admit it now. He'd been so damn scared she wouldn't come. But she was here. And together they could work through anything.

Phoebe looked at him through the glass, her expression unreadable. When she reached the restaurant door, she hesitated, then turned and kept walking.

"That was Phoebe. Wasn't that Phoebe? Did she just walk by?" Naomi asked, clearly perplexed.

Ryan grunted. His gut response was to rush outside, haul her stubborn butt home and screw her to the point of exhaustion so she'd agree to marry him. But he'd already tried that, after a fashion, and it hadn't worked.

"Cancel the salad and I'll take the stromboli now." It was pretty damn amazing how calm and composed he sounded when he was dying inside.

Naomi sniffled and swiped at a tear. "Those are the saddest words I've ever heard."

Ryan couldn't agree more.

POEBE TURNED her chair and stared at the Nashville skyline showcased by her office window. This view at dusk, when the city lights flickered like fireflies against the encroaching darkness, always thrilled her.

It failed to thrill her now. She swivelled around. She felt dead inside. Dead and empty. But that was preferable to hurting so damn bad she could barely tolerate the pain. That's what lurked behind her emptiness. The emptiness merely held the pain at bay. But it kept things manageable. She closed her eyes. Was this what the rest of her life would be like? Managed emptiness? Perhaps. She'd felt this way before, every time her parents promised to come get her and had never shown up. It wasn't a new sensation. But before, Ryan had always helped her through. Now there was no Ryan.

Phoebe pulled on her coat, picked up her briefcase and locked her door behind her. Moving on autopilot, she rode the elevator down to the parking garage, found her car and joined the steady stream of rush-hour commuters.

Red taillights stretched ahead of her. It had been five long weeks since she'd met Ryan at the park. Five weeks of feeling as if an important part of her was missing. Was he right? Did she deliberately hold everyone at arm's length? She'd always thought her reserve was a part of her personality. But there'd been nothing reserved about the passion she'd found within herself in Jamaica.

Lost in thought, Phoebe tuned in and realized she was a block from Aunt Caroline's house. In the slow flow of traffic, she'd found her way to the place that had offered her refuge since childhood. She'd produced one reason or another to avoid Caroline's repeated dinner invitations in the last month. She hadn't wanted to discuss Jamaica with her aunt. She'd told herself it was because she didn't want anyone close to her to know about her and Ryan. But maybe only part of that was right—maybe she just didn't want anyone close to her.

She parked her car in the driveway and approached the Depression-era bungalow with a sense of homecoming. She bypassed the front door and wound her way to the back stoop. The familiar clink of metal against stone resounded from the open door of the detached two-car garage that served as Uncle Frank's studio.

Phoebe opened the back door that led straight into the kitchen. Aunt Caroline sat at a corner desk, surfing the Internet, a glass of wine on her desk. Two salads sat ready on the kitchen table, crowded by a stack of magazines and newspapers and junk mail.

"Hi."

Aunt Caroline whirled around, joy lighting her angular face. "Phoebe! We've missed you so. We were beginning to think you didn't love us." She pushed away from the computer and started across the room, her spontaneous smile giving way to a frown of concern, her footsteps flagging. "Sugar, what's the matter?"

Phoebe hadn't planned to wind up here. Nor did she plan to burst into tears and fling herself into Aunt Caroline's open arms. Nonetheless, that's where she found herself. Sobs racked her, rendering her incoherent. Aunt Caroline held her tight against her spare frame, rocking the two of them back and forth in a soothing motion but making no effort to stem the tide of emotion ripping Phoebe apart.

Finally, the storm inside her subsided. Embarrassed, desperately in need of a box of tissues, she pulled back from the comfort of Caroline's arms and tried to stumble through an apology, "I'm sorry—"

Caroline would have none of it. She smoothed

Phoebe's hair and pushed her into a kitchen chair. "Don't you dare apologize, my sweet, sweet girl."

Phoebe snuffled and tried to compose herself. Caroline turned from the sink with a damp paper towel. She blotted away Phoebe's residual tears, the paper cool and calming against her heated skin. Then as if Phoebe were six instead of thirty, Caroline handed her the paper towel and instructed, "Blow."

Phoebe blew. And sat there at a loss. She really hadn't planned to come over and she didn't know what to say. She drew a deep shuddering breath. "I didn't mean to—"

Caroline cut her off again, her eyes awash with tears. "Shh. Do you know how long I've waited for you to come to me for anything? I hate it that you're unhappy, but I'm glad you're here. I've waited a lifetime for this." Guilt and sorrow painted her face, "Of course, that's the way it's always been."

"What are you talking about, Aunt Caroline?" Phoebe spoke softly, surprised by the pain etching her aunt's usually cheery face.

"Your uncle Frank and I found out we couldn't have children a few years after we were married."

Phoebe started in surprise. She'd always assumed they didn't want children.

"It probably wouldn't be a big deal today, but thirty-five years ago, they didn't know nearly as much about infertility and we didn't have the money to spend the thousands of dollars to pursue it," her aunt continued.

She paused, closing her eyes for a second as if seeking the words to continue. She looked up. "And then Lynette and Vance had you." Love transformed and softened Caroline's angular face. It took Phoebe a second to realize it was love for her. "You were wonderful. Bright and beautiful, and I tried very hard to be happy for Lynette and Vance." Her voice broke. "They were so careless with you. Living like Gypsies, going wherever their wanderlust led them. So many nights I worried that you didn't have enough to eat or a place to stay."

Even now, sitting in the warmth of Caroline's kitchen, Phoebe instantly recalled going to bed and waking up in the back seat of her parent's car with a gnawing hunger eating at her empty belly. She knew her confirmation would only hurt Caroline. She held her tongue.

"You were so smart. But they never stayed in one place long enough to enroll you in kindergarten or first grade. When they left you with us, Phoebe, I was glad." She spoke with a fierceness Phoebe had never heard in her voice before. "I was ashamed then and I'm ashamed now at how happy I was over something that caused you so much pain. You were a gift to us, a blessing we never expected. I kept thinking that one day, if we gave you enough space and showed you we loved you, you'd come to accept us and love us in return. I'm so sorry, Phoebe, but I thought you were better off with us. I never kept Lynette and Vance away, but I never pushed them to come for you, either. Because I wanted you for my own."

Tears rolled down Caroline's face. Fat, silent tears that picked up momentum. Without giving it consideration, Phoebe pushed away from the table and stood, wrapping her arms around Caroline.

They'd wanted her. All this time, they'd wanted *her.* She wasn't an obligation. She was a blessing. "I thought you all didn't want me but were too kindhearted to send away a stray. God knows, you had enough strays already."

"Do you remember Boris, the big tomcat that wandered up the spring you got your braces?"

"Yes." Boris had trusted no one and tolerated few.

"You were so like Boris. Do you remember how you'd put food out and watch him eat? Every day you'd get a little bit closer, but he never would let you touch him. But then he and Duchess became friends, and you stopped trying to pet him because he wasn't alone anymore."

Phoebe nodded. She'd desperately wanted Boris to let her near him.

"You were like that cat. Skittish and standoffish, but you and Ryan found one another so Frank and I figured you were okay. Although we never stopped wanting you to let us near you."

Phoebe never realized how much her distance had hurt them. "I'm so sorry."

"Honey, it's hard to learn to trust and open yourself up. It's hard to believe you won't find yourself abandoned again. We probably should've found a therapist to help you deal with everything. But the money was always tight and we thought if we just loved you enough, one day you'd let us love you."

Phoebe felt like a dike with a small hole that couldn't withstand the relentless pressure of water on the other side. Caroline's words crumbled the wall that had surrounded Phoebe's heart for as long as she could recall.

"Why?" One word. So important. "Why didn't they want me, Aunt Caroline?"

"I don't know why." Compassion lit Caroline's eyes. "I've never figured it out. Maybe it's because Lynette was the youngest and our parents spoiled her. Maybe it's just the way she is. But you'll find out as you go through life that often there's no ready answer as to why. Things just are, and we have to deal with them."

"That's not good enough. I need the whys."

"Forget about the why and get on with life. I think you've already come up with your own why, and you're wrong. Look at me, Phoebe, when I tell you this." She cupped Phoebe's chin in a gentle hand. "Your parents dropped you off and never came back. They deserved a horsewhipping for that. And a good flogging still wouldn't cover all the times they told you they'd be there and never were. But the thing you need to know is, there's something wrong with *them*. Not with you. My guess is that some time ago, you decided you didn't care and wouldn't let them hurt you anymore."

"They can't hurt me anymore."

"They can't as soon as you wrestle control of your life from them."

"They have absolutely no control over me."

"Unfortunately, they do. You're still letting them control you. You're still giving them the power. Your fear of abandonment, the fear to let someone get too close to you—that's the power you've given them over your life. If you don't move past that, you'll never realize your full potential. You only get out of life what you put into it. And life can be so good for you. Don't let them cripple you." Caroline paused as if carefully considering her next words, "And don't let them ruin what you could have with Ryan."

Phoebe dropped back into her chair. "What about Ryan?"

"He called us a few weeks ago. He loves you, Phoebe. He's so in love with you he can hardly stand himself. Just like you love him. Frank and I have seen it for years."

"But all his girlfriends—all those relationships..."

"Phoebe, those were never relationships. That was a man doing what a man does best, running scared. If you look beneath all of his easygoing charm, Ryan's a Boris, too. His mother chose to drink herself to death, and then his father flitted from woman to woman and never paid Ryan any attention. That boy was as abandoned as you. He doesn't trust easily, either. But from the day you met, you were the Duchess to his Boris. I've never seen two people more destined for one another and take longer to figure it out."

Phoebe sat for a minute, absorbing Caroline's words.

The fear inside her fought them. "Why didn't you tell me this sooner?"

"Because your heart wasn't ready to hear it."

"But what if—"

Caroline laid a quieting hand on her shoulder. "Life doesn't come with any guarantees, Phoebe. All you can do is love like there's no tomorrow and hope for the best."

Moving past the repression she'd spent years perfecting, Phoebe hugged Caroline. Holding her aunt near, she found the courage to give voice to the words she'd never been able to say before. "I love you."

BRIDGETTE FOLLOWED her as Phoebe dug the cardboard shoe box out of the back of her closet and carried it into her living room. Her hand trembled when she removed the worn lid. It was a time capsule of sorts, she supposed.

She pulled out a dog-eared photo. Twenty-five years ago. A pensive Phoebe stood sandwiched between her laughing parents in a grainy color Polaroid. She remembered that day as clearly as if it were yesterday.

She showed Bridgette the photo. "There we are, girl. We'd stopped at a roadside circus. They were having a great time, but I was tired and hungry." They'd spent the night in their car, and according to her parents, there hadn't been enough money for breakfast. Of course, there'd been money for the circus.

How many times had she wondered over the years, each time she looked at the photo, if they'd left her behind because she wasn't fun enough? Smart enough? Pretty enough? Lovable enough? Had she complained about being tired and hungry too much? Because she had been, quite often.

She'd wondered far more times than she cared to remember. It had become a visible cue for inadequacy. Where had she fallen short of the mark? She consciously stemmed the feelings as they welled up inside her.

Bridgette settled her head in Phoebe's lap, as if to offer comfort, her brown eyes solemn, trusting and full of love. Phoebe looked at her. Why had someone dropped Bridgette off at the pound? Phoebe had wondered for a long time. She'd spent the first several months watching for bad behavior, some clue as to why someone wouldn't want a great dog like Bridgette. And finally, over the course of time, she'd stopped wondering. Bridgette was wonderful, and Phoebe loved her. Thank goodness they'd found one another.

She placed the photo on the couch and pulled out a handful of papers. Poems, notes, unmailed envelopes. Outpourings of her adolescent confusion, outrage, humiliation, bitterness. All on paper. Saved to be presented one day to her parents.

An infinite sadness welled inside her. This had been such a central part of her life for so long, it was hard to let it go. She sat on the floor before the fireplace, the crackling fire spreading heat and light.

Her hand shook as she tentatively fed the first envelope into the fire. As the flames licked and curled across the envelope, consuming it, a tear trickled down her face, and Phoebe felt a release. With each piece of paper, it became easier and the tears flowed faster. Sobbing, she tossed the box and the lid into the grate. The fire whooshed as it greedily devoured them.

Bridgette nuzzled against her and barked at the flames.

The only remnant from the box was the photo. Phoebe picked it up, holding its worn corner between her thumb and forefinger, offering it up, as well.

At the last moment she snatched it back. All the bitterness, all the hurt were gone. But she still needed to remember who she was and where she'd come from. She could look at the photo and know that why was no longer important. Her heart had finally heard the message.

RYAN couldn't seem to break himself of the habit of showing up at Birelli's each Thursday. Even though it had been five long weeks since Phoebe had stopped coming. Instead of watching for her, he spent his lunch hour reading reports.

Naomi appeared out of nowhere and sloshed a sweet tea opposite him, a huge grin on her face.

"Earth to Naomi. I already have a drink."

"Yeah. But she doesn't."

He looked up and his heart damn near stopped. Phoebe stood inside the doorway looking strong, yet vulnerable. His eyes never left her face as she made her way across the room. Time had pronounced the hollows beneath her cheekbones and the faint shadows beneath her eyes.

She stopped at the table, tugging on the strap of her shoulderbag. "Mind if I sit down?"

"It's your spot."

Phoebe slid onto the stool. Naomi beamed at her. "I'll be right back with a salad."

"Wait. I'll have the spinach and chicken stromboli."

"But you always have the salad."

"I know. But it's the stromboli that I always want. So, I'll have that."

"Sure thing." Naomi's smile was blinding as she hurried off.

An awkward silence settled between them. Were they friends? Lovers? Uneasy acquaintances? Hell if he knew. The only thing he knew for sure was that he loved her and he'd missed her like crazy. He'd already stepped out on a limb twice and been knocked off. What was the saying about the third time being a charm? Of course there was the three strikes and you're out deal, too. He figured, either way, he didn't have anything to lose that he hadn't already lost. Pride was a small matter these days.

"So, did you come to tell me you want to marry me?"

"Well, as a matter of fact I did." She lifted her chin in defiance.

He needed to know what had changed her mind. "Why?"

"Why do I want to marry you?" She shoved her hair behind her ear with an unsteady hand.

"Yeah. Why now?" Would she see this through or bolt like some wild, frightened animal?

"It's the only way I can get you to have sex with me." She offered a tenuous smile.

"There is that." She'd regained her sense of humor. That was a start.

"I love you." Her words were so quiet, he almost missed them.

"But you loved me before, and it wasn't enough for you then."

She took his hand in hers and brought it to her mouth, her breath warm against him. It was as if she'd brought him back to life after weeks of only existing.

"I'm not scared anymore, Ryan. I'm not scared to love you and I'm not scared to let you love me."

"How do I know you won't get scared again?" A man could only be resurrected so many times. "When I stumbled across you in those woods, twenty-something years ago, you brought me back to life. I had been hurting for months. You made me whole. Being apart from you these last several weeks...I can't go through that again, Phoebes."

"You have to trust me. Just like I have to trust you. I want to grow old with you. I need you. You're the ebb and flow in my ocean. You bring the change to my life that I need."

"Just like you're the sand on my shore, my anchor, my constant."

Ryan reached in his pants pocket and pulled out the small square box he'd brought home from Jamaica and had carried every day since. He felt ridiculously nervous.

She opened the box and found the simply designed ring of two strands of metal, intertwined, unbroken, linked forever. He felt her pleasure in the link that had always connected them. "It's beautiful."

He wrapped his hand around the nape of her neck beneath the silky fall of her hair and pulled her closer, his body thrumming in response to her scent that had haunted him. "We can look for a diamond—"

"No. This is what I want. When did you get it?" Her mouth was tantalizingly close to his.

"When we were in Jamaica. The afternoon before I proposed that night. Martin had a—"

She laughed, her warm breath soothing him. "Let me guess. Martin had a cousin that works in a jewelry shop."

"How'd you know?" She had the most perfect lips.

"I think Martin's very well-connected," she murmured as her hand cupped his jaw and her mouth found his.

It was a fairly chaste kiss of promise that, nonetheless, sent the fire of desire licking through him. Phoebe pulled away, her eyes reflecting the same need he felt. "I have something for you, as well."

She pulled an envelope out of her handbag and placed it on the table before him. Ryan pulled out two

Air Jamaica tickets and a Hot Sands honeymoon suite confirmation.

Private pools. Sunsets. Long hot days and longer, hotter nights. Tension coiled deep inside him. "You were that sure of me?"

She shook her head. "No. I was that sure of us. I wasn't going to give you up."

Naomi stopped by with the stromboli.

"Can we get those to go?"

Naomi picked the plates up with a knowing smile. "Sure thing. Want me to throw in a baklava or two?"

"That's okay. I think we'll pick up some chocolate-covered doughnuts along the way."

_____Epilogue_____

Three months later

"Welcome back to Jamaica. It is most excellent to see you again." A genuine smile wreathed Martin's face.

"It's lovely to be back." Phoebe was delighted to see him.

"We're here on our honeymoon," Ryan announced. The same way he'd announced it to anyone who'd listen since they'd said their "I do's" this morning.

Martin pumped Ryan's hand and then Phoebe's. "Did you have the wedding here in our lovely gazebo by the sea?" Martin asked.

"No. We got married in Nashville so our families could attend." It had been important to Phoebe to have Aunt Caroline and Uncle Frank present. Both had cried when she'd asked Uncle Frank to walk her down the aisle. They'd skipped, however, the giving away part. She loved her family but she was no one's to give away. "We would have definitely invited you and Mathilde if we'd tied the knot here."

"Ah, it is so romantic." Martin swiped at a tear. "It is the island magic. Just like me and my Mathilde."

Phoebe smiled, her heart full. You had to love a man

who was a sappy sentimentalist. She certainly loved Ryan, and he fit the bill.

Ryan rubbed his hand in small circular motions against her back. "How are Mathilde and the kids?"

"Most excellent. I am a very rich man, you know."

She leaned into the hard length of Ryan's body, absorbing his scent and his heat. "Yes, I do know. I've just become a very rich woman."

"It would be an honor if you would allow me to prepare a special table tonight along with a special menu, if you can take a late seating. My cousin, he is now a chef here."

Laughter sparkled in Ryan's eyes as he glanced at Phoebe. "We'd like that. We're definitely not dressed for dinner now, and we'd still like to walk on the beach."

"Ah. You are fond of our spectacular sunsets, then?"

A long look, full of memories and promise, passed between Ryan and Phoebe. Heat that refused to be cooled by the ocean breeze filled her. "Yes, we're both fond of your sunsets. They're quite—"

"Exhilarating," Ryan finished for her. A wicked smile pulled his dimple into full play and weakened her knees.

"Most excellent. I look forward to serving you then. Enjoy your sunset."

Phoebe's heart pounded in time with the steel drums as she and Ryan left the restaurant and stepped onto the sugar-fine sand. Her simple white dress left her legs bare to the last slanting rays of the sinking sun and the whisper of the ocean breeze. Ryan clasped her hand in his as they walked along the shoreline, the translucent blue water lapping at their ankles. She glanced at him, his green eyes full of heat and promise.

The sun sank lower until it lost itself between the lines of earth and sky, painting both in vivid oranges and soft pinks. On a secluded section of Jamaican beach she'd come to regard as their own, Phoebe lost herself in the warmth of Ryan's arms and the heat of his kiss.

Bathed in twilight and the warm waters of the Caribbean, Ryan eased her down into the surf.

"It's not dark yet," she murmured, more observation than objection.

His hand cupped her breast. His finger brushed her nipple through her dress as he nibbled along her neck. "I know."

"You know what this is?" She tugged his shirttail free and slid her hands against the hair-roughened plane of his belly, her breath coming in short, sharp pants. She wanted him as fiercely as she had the first time. She thought it would always be this way between them—hot and needy and "...barely decent."

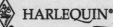
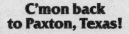

Blaze

HARLEQUIN® *Blaze*™

Bare Essentials

Bare Essentials—Revenge has never been *this* good!

Kate Jones and Cassie Montgomery have a few scores to settle with their hometown. When they turn their attentions to the town's tempting first son and the sexy sheriff, temperatures rise and things start getting interesting....

#62 *NATURALLY NAUGHTY*
by Leslie Kelly

#63 *NAUGHTY, BUT NICE*
by Jill Shalvis

Don't miss these red-hot, linked stories from Leslie Kelly and Jill Shalvis!

*Both books available November 2002
at your favorite retail outlet.*

HARLEQUIN®
Makes any time special ®

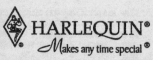

If you enjoyed what you just read,
then we've got an offer you can't resist!

Take 2 bestselling
love stories FREE!

Plus get a FREE surprise gift!

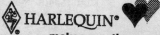
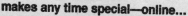
HINTMAG